"Someone just tried to kill you," Emmett said.

"I'm not leaving until I check out your apartment," he added.

Relenting, she led the way to her apartment. She opened the door and stepped inside, almost stumbling on a yellow envelope.

His gaze moved from the envelope to Belle. "Were you expecting mail?"

"Not shoved underneath my door, no."

Emmett picked up the envelope with a tissue and Belle found latex gloves so she could open it.

The handwritten scribbles said it all.

I intend to finish what I started. You ruined my life. I intend to ruin yours. Maybe I'll find one of your sisters next.

TRUE BLUE K-9 UNIT: BROOKLYN

These police officers fight for justice
with the help of their brave canine partners.

With over seventy books published and millions in print, **Lenora Worth** writes award-winning romance and romantic suspense. Three of her books finaled in the ACFW Carol Awards, and her Love Inspired Suspense novel *Body of Evidence* became a *New York Times* bestseller. Her novella in *Mistletoe Kisses* made her a *USA TODAY* bestselling author. Lenora goes on adventures with her retired husband, Don, and enjoys reading, baking and shopping... especially shoe shopping.

Visit the Author Profile page at Harlequin.com for more titles.

DEADLY CONNECTION

LENORA WORTH

LOVE INSPIRED SUSPENSE
INSPIRATIONAL ROMANCE

Special thanks and acknowledgment are given to Lenora Worth for her contribution to the True Blue K-9 Unit: Brooklyn miniseries.

LOVE INSPIRED® SUSPENSE
INSPIRATIONAL ROMANCE

ISBN-13: 978-1-335-40284-4

Recycling programs for this product may not exist in your area.

Deadly Connection

Copyright © 2020 by Harlequin Books S.A.

This edition published by arrangement with Harlequin Books S.A.

For questions and comments about the quality of this book, please contact us at CustomerService@Harlequin.com.

Love Inspired
22 Adelaide St. West, 40th Floor
Toronto, Ontario M5H 4E3, Canada
www.Harlequin.com

Printed in U.S.A.

Have not I commanded thee? Be strong and of a good courage; be not afraid, neither be thou dismayed: for the Lord thy God is with thee whithersoever thou goest.
–Joshua 1:9

To Brooklyn, New York. Thanks for letting me visit
in my imagination. Thanks also to the NYPD
for working to keep one of my favorite cities safe.

ONE

Brooklyn K-9 Unit Officer Belle Montera glanced back on the shortcut through Cadman Plaza Park, her K-9 partner, Justice, a sleek German shepherd, moving ahead of her as she held tightly to his leash. She had a weird sense she was being followed, but it had to be nothing. Checking her watch, she noted it was almost 5:00 p.m. Still plenty of summer light left, but the skies were darkening with the threat of an afternoon thunderstorm. Brooklyn in the summer—always full of surprises. Rain showers could be one of those.

Belle was used to the ever-changing weather and she was used to keeping her radar on full speed. She always felt safe in her city, but she never let her guard down, either.

Justice lifted his black nose and sniffed the humid air, then gave a soft woof. He might have seen a squirrel frolicking in the tall oaks, or he could have sensed Belle's agitation. Still on duty, she kept a keen eye on her surroundings. Justice could always use the exercise, and she loved having him with her all the time, but this was official business.

"No time to go after innocent squirrels," she told Justice. "We're working, remember?"

Her faithful companion gave her a dark-eyed stare, his black K-9 unit protective vest cinched around his firm belly.

They were both on high alert.

Her service weapon sat nestled in its holster around her duty belt, her NYPD badge shone on her black uniform shirt and her partner was highly trained in protection.

The entire department had been a little antsy lately, so no wonder she had a trace of the jitters.

This meeting could provide the lead the Brooklyn K-9 Unit had been waiting for. A recent double homicide had been eerily similar to one that had taken place twenty years ago in Bay Ridge. Thanks to new technology, evidence in the cold case—an old leather watchband—had finally provided DNA on the killer. If this meeting panned out, Belle could help the unit get closer to finding that killer. *And* if he'd struck again two months ago.

Sergeant Gavin Sutherland, the head of their unit, had warned her to be careful. He'd explained to the entire team that their suspect perp could be watching and waiting. Two members of their K-9 unit, brother and sister Bradley and Penelope McGregor, lost their parents in that twenty-year-old cold case, and either the killer had returned or they had a copycat on their hands. The team needed to stay alert.

Belle intended to do just that.

"It's okay, boy," she said, giving Justice's shiny black-and-tan coat a soft rub. "Just my overactive imagination getting the best of me."

She had a meeting with a man who could have information regarding the McGregor murders. The DNA match from that case had indicated that US Marshal Emmett Gage could be related to the killer.

The team had done a thorough background check on the marshal to eliminate him as a suspect, then Belle had been assigned to meet with him.

Justice lifted his head and sniffed again, his nose in the air. The big dog glanced back. Belle checked over her shoulder.

No one there.

After a few years as a beat cop and now one year into working as an Emergency Services officer, Belle had cross-trained to be tough and unemotional no matter the situation. But added to the grueling training, sometimes her anxieties kicked in and turned things up a notch. Since she did have good instincts in spite of those anxieties, she slowed and listened to hear if any footsteps hit the strip of pavement curving through the path toward the federal courthouse near the park.

But the only sounds were the birds chirping in the rustling trees and the swish of a hot summer breeze moving over her skin. The never-ending traffic noise echoed out over the trees and distant laughter followed but, for the most part, she was alone on this path. Rain clouds formed overhead while humidity covered her clothes and moistened the short ponytail at the nape of her neck.

Slowing her pace, Belle listened. She heard through the trees what sounded like a motorcycle revving, then nothing but the birds chirping. Minutes passed and then she heard a noise on the path, the crackle of a twig breaking, the slight shift of shoes hitting asphalt, a whiff of stale body odor wafting through the air. The hair on the back of her neck stood up and Belle knew then.

Someone is following me.

Justice let out an aggressive growl and Belle turned around, ready to draw her hidden Sig Sauer pistol. Nothing there. No one behind her. Maybe a jogger who'd left the path?

This time, she heard footfalls in the thick underbrush just off the trail. No doubt someone moved close behind. But were they after her or just taking a different route?

A swoosh of air hissed by. A silencer?

Belle waited for the impact of a bullet but instead she heard Justice let out a soft whine. Then her beautiful, brave partner fell over on his side, a tranquilizer dart sticking out of his right shoulder. He lifted his head and whimpered, his eyes beseeching. Then he passed out, his head dropping.

"No," Belle screamed. "No, Justice, no. Get up, boy."

Belle knelt next to Justice and scanned the woods and paths. Before she could get a fix on who had shot the tranquilizer, big hands grabbed her from behind and squeezed at her midsection, knocking the air out of her lungs. A sweaty man pulled her up against his chest, his hand moist and rancid-smelling over her mouth, his big signet ring digging against her skin. "Now you'll pay for what you did."

Using all of her might, Belle grunted and tried to trip her captor, but he slapped at her and then flipped her around to face him. He wore a black baseball-style hat and dark shades. She fought to get free while she studied his face, but he held her back and then shoved his hands around her neck.

Choking, Belle tried to grab at his hands but the pressure of his splayed fingers digging into her neck and cutting off her air supply caused her head to swim. Stars pricked at her eyes. Fighting against him, Belle knew she'd faint soon, and he'd finish the job. She tried again to save herself, kicking at him, but he shifted back.

She grasped his sweaty shirt and raked her fingernails down the thin dark material, hoping to save some DNA. That gave her an opportunity to smash her heavy black boot against his left foot, bearing down enough that he screamed in pain. With all her might, she tried to free her arms so she could get to her weapon.

But he didn't let go. Instead, the angry brute applied more pressure as he shoved her down to the hard asphalt and held her throat, his grunts matching each increase of force against her neck and windpipe.

She blinked, kicked, wished Justice would wake up and attack. Prayed she'd be able to use what strength she had left to get this brute's hands off her neck. But the stars bursting against her skull like a sci-fi war began to explode with pain now.

She wasn't going to make it. This man was going to get the best of her if she didn't find one last measure of force. With a grunt that took every bit of her strength, she shifted her body and dropped both her hands to her side, causing him to think he'd finally done her in. When he released the pressure, Belle reached for her weapon. The man pushed at her arm, making her unable to shoot. She slammed the weapon hard against his head.

He yelled and blinked, rage turning his olive skin red. Knocking her gun loose, he sent it flying onto the grass. "You just made your last mistake." His hands renewed their assault and this time, Belle had no energy left to fight.

But somewhere through the ringing in her ears, Belle heard a shout. "US Marshal! Let go of the woman and show me your hands."

The man stopped, his nasty clammy fingers lifting away from her neck, his grunt of frustration loud. He looked down at Belle, rage pouring off him along with sweat. Belle blinked and started coughing.

The man who'd shouted at her attacker inched his way closer and repeated, "I said get away from the officer. Now."

Her attacker crouched near and gave her one last hostile glare, then shot up and spun away. Still disoriented, she heard a grunt and then realized he had pulled out a gun. As a last resort if choking her wasn't going to work?

Belle tried to get to where he'd tossed her weapon but shots rang out, causing her to throw herself over Justice. The man took off running into the nearby woods, shooting backward toward her and her rescuer before he scrambled into the heavy thicket.

Then she heard the sound again. A motor revving. The same motorcycle she'd heard earlier?

"You all right?" the marshal asked as he ran toward her.

"Sí," she managed to croak out. "Yes," she repeated, her shocked brain registering her lapse into Spanish. This man had to be her contact. "Go. Find him."

He took off, but Belle knew the perpetrator was probably long gone. She crawled toward her weapon, then hurried back to Justice.

Belle clung to the dog, more concerned about her partner right now than the man getting away. She thought she had a good description of her attacker and she'd remember that chunky ring jabbing against her skin. How would she ever get his angry expression and the feel of his beefy hands out of her system?

"Justice." She knew he'd have to sleep this off, but she prayed it wasn't worse. Her partner had to wake up. They'd been together since day one. She trusted this loyal shepherd with her life and today she'd let him down by not being as diligent as she should have been.

Her hands shaking, she reached for her cell to call for backup.

Before she could get her bearings, the man who'd gone after her attacker came crashing through the underbrush and then kneeled down beside her, his phone to his ear. "US Marshal Emmett Gage. Need backup and an ambulance at Cadman Plaza Park. Assault on a police officer, shots fired. Suspect headed west into wooded area north of Tillary."

"Motorcycle," she whispered. "I heard one."

Emmett repeated to the dispatcher what she'd told him.

"Justice needs help," Belle gasped, her throat raw with pain while she pointed to the big shepherd. "Ask for veterinary help. Tell them I'm Brooklyn K-9 Unit Officer Belle Montera, Emergency Services, and that my partner, Justice, was hit with a tranquilizer dart."

The man beside her gave her a surprised stare but reported her words to the dispatcher. Then he put the phone on speaker while he checked her over, his steel-blue eyes burning her like a laser, his frown set in place and his demeanor nothing but professional. "Victim has ligature marks around her neck and bruises to her face and hands. Eyes somewhat bloodshot. Hurry."

Belle took in deep breaths while she studied US Marshal Emmett Gage. His official photo didn't do him justice. Once they'd found him as a match to the DNA, she'd immediately vetted the man. Tall with stormy blue eyes and hair the color of dry wheat. Stoic, standoffish and serious—that's how people described the man. But one of the best in doing his job. He'd helped hunt down and bring in dangerous fugitives from all over the country.

He looked tough and no-nonsense and she immediately felt better. No, she felt safe. Up until this moment, Belle had always taken care of herself. But right now, she allowed this man to comfort her. Shock. She had to be in shock from the attack.

Trying to focus while the marshal at her side stayed on the phone, Belle went over the case to calm her frantic mind.

Penelope and Bradley McGregor, her colleagues—Penny the front desk clerk and Bradley a K-9 detective, deserved justice for their parents' murders, which had gone unsolved for so long. As did little Lucy Emery, whose parents were killed with the same MO on the twentieth anniversary of the McGregor murders. Like toddler Lucy, Penny, then four, had been spared by the killer, disguised in a clown mask and blue wig. Lucy was an only child, but Penny's brother, Bradley, had been sleeping over at a friend's house the night of the homicides, and the fourteen-year-old had been unfairly deemed a suspect for too long. The recent murders had brought up all kinds of questions and, so far, very few answers.

Tonight, despite almost being killed herself, Belle still planned to interrogate Emmett Gage.

Now, she could vouch for how the people she'd questioned had described Emmett. His calm radiated a commanding respect, but he seemed as tightly coiled as a giant snake and ready to strike. Yet he managed to hold all that power in check while he tried to keep her calm and watch his own back at the same time.

His voice went low and husky when his gaze softened on her as if she were the only person in the world. "Backup's on the way."

He checked Justice, rubbing the still animal's stomach. "His pulse is weak, but I'm guessing the tranquilizer won't keep him down long." Lifting his chin toward the dart, he added, "Your lab can analyze this to see what they used. The dispatcher said they'd get in touch with the unit's official vet."

Touched that he'd been concerned, Belle nodded and tried to speak. Then she pushed with her bruised, burning hands on the gritty walkway and tried to stand. But she promptly plopped back down into a sitting position, the dizziness swirling inside her head making her nauseous.

"Don't," he said, steadying her. "You'll be hoarse for a while and your shoulders and neck will hurt and be sore. A lot. You might have fuzzy memories and nightmares for a brief time, too. Strangulation is nothing to take lightly."

She swallowed, wishing she had some cold water. "You've been choked before?" she asked on a whisper.

He let out what might have been a chopped-up chuckle. "One or two times when I've wrestled with junkies full of drugs and adrenaline."

Pushing at her lopsided ponytail, she croaked, "He got the jump on me."

His eyes softened. "Don't like that, huh?"

She shook her head, mortified that she hadn't managed to shake her attacker. "I'm usually more prepared."

With a curt nod, he stood and searched around for any evidence of who might have attacked her. Then he sank down beside her as sirens shrilled in the distance. "You were headed to meet me, right?"

She nodded. "I need—"

"We'll discuss that later," he responded, getting up to wave to the EMTs and the patrol officer running toward them. "Right now, let's get you and your partner some help."

Belle could only keep nodding as *her* adrenaline rush slowly began to sink down while the shakes took over. She wouldn't let anyone see her falling apart but she did feel an overwhelming gratitude toward Emmett Gage.

The man she'd come here to interrogate had just saved her life.

Emmett kept a close eye on the woman impatiently waiting for the paramedics to return from giving Gavin a report so she could sign off on no further treatment. She tapped her hands against the ambulance door and strained her neck to see what was holding them up.

To keep her calm, he started talking. "I live in Dumbo, but I got home late. If I'd left a few minutes earlier—"

"He might have shot you," she said on a raw whisper. Then she looked up at him with eyes the color of dark rich wood. "Thank you for helping me with Justice. I need to make sure he'll be all right."

Emmett glanced to where the dog had been moved off the path. "He should be fine. Might be off his game for a few days, though."

"I think we'll both need to debrief," she replied, checking on the still-unconscious K-9 again.

When she moved to get up, Emmett held her back. "He's sleeping. You need to sit here for a minute."

"I'm not good at sitting," she admitted. Giving him a questioning glance, she asked, "So you know why I wanted to talk to you, right?"

Emmett nodded. "I wasn't late in an attempt to put off talking to you. I got held up with some red tape regarding a case we just closed."

"But you had good timing, anyway," she said on a husky whisper, each word forced through pain.

"Thankful for that," he replied, taking his time in studying her. Her dark hair shimmered in the waning sunshine, but her eyes went dark each time she glanced at the still canine beside her.

Belle fidgeted and glanced around again. "Why are the paramedics still talking to Sarge? I told them when they examined me earlier, I'm fine."

"You should go to the hospital."

"No. I can't leave Justice." She stood and leaned on the back of the ambulance, clearly not happy. "I can sign off. I don't need anything. Is our veterinarian on her way?"

"I heard your sergeant say she is," Emmett told Belle, thinking the officer was single-minded about her partner. A good trait, but he wished he could reassure her about the canine. "Bringing her van and a special wheeled cot to get Justice back to her office in the K-9 training center. He'll have his own dog-sized gurney."

He offered Belle some water and she took a tentative sip, then said, "I want to go straight there."

Emmett didn't argue with her, but he figured the K-9 would sleep most of the night. "Then I'll make sure you get there." When he glanced up and saw an auburn-haired female wearing silver glasses approaching with a small rolling cot, Emmett touched Belle's arm. "I think your vet is here."

Belle's head shot up as she hurried toward the veterinarian, her anxious eyes showing fatigue and concern.

While Belle talked to the doctor, Emmett thought back over the meeting they hadn't had yet.

Worry gnawed at his gut while he wondered about her. According to the request that had come into his office, she needed to verify the hit the NYPD had received that revealed *his* DNA matched the sample found on a watchband that had been collected as evidence at the cold-case murder site. Emmett could probably answer her question without a doubt. The DNA might be a match for his, but twenty years ago, he'd been twelve years old, living in South Brooklyn with his parents and grandparents, all of whom were dead now.

The Brooklyn K-9 Unit needed information on the unknown relative he'd matched and since he only had one living relative who could have possibly been in the area, he was pretty sure he knew who they were looking for.

Randall Gage. But he couldn't picture his dad's cousin Randall as a murderer. Always in trouble and always with one foot in the fire, yes. But capable of murder? What if Randall was? How would Emmett handle that?

Emmett wanted to get to the bottom of this and fast.

But first he needed to convince Belle Montera that she should go home and rest. Or go somewhere close. His place wasn't far from here. Taking her there, however, might turn out to be more difficult than tracking the fugitive he'd been chasing over the last two days. She'd balk at that suggestion.

From the way Belle was questioning the calm, patient veterinarian, he had a feeling she'd rather be with her partner right now than find out any facts from Emmett. The woman had been almost choked to death and her partner had been tranquilized. She was still in shock and worried about her K-9.

"Let me help, Dr. Mazelli," he said when the tiny woman tried to lift the dog. Justice had to weigh at least eighty pounds.

"Thank you," Dr. Mazelli said. "Belle should go home. Based on whatever was in that dart, Justice should wake up in an hour or so but he'll be too groggy to notice anything, so it's best if he has some quiet time. He should be fine tomorrow, but we'll keep him off duty for a couple of days to be sure."

"You might want to convince Officer Montera of that," Emmett replied. "She's insisting she wants to stay the night with him."

After they'd lifted Justice up onto the cart, the doctor went over to where Belle stood talking to Sergeant Sutherland.

The vet touched the officer's arm and told her in a gentle tone that the best thing she could do was get some rest. "Justice will be fine with me. I won't leave him alone, Belle, I promise. You need to take care of yourself."

"Do as she suggests," Gavin told Belle as Emmett came hurrying up to them. "That's an order."

"But, sir—"

"Rest, Belle," Gavin added.

"I'll get her home," Emmett said, daring anyone to argue with him. He and Gavin had been officially introduced earlier so he hoped he wasn't overstepping.

The tough-looking sergeant stared him down, then said in a gruff voice, "Good idea. You two have some unfinished business, anyway. And when you're done, I'd like a full report."

Sutherland didn't give Belle time to argue. He marched off to talk to the other K-9 officers moving across the park. When her unit had heard the call coming through, they'd all come to assist. Dedicated and tenacious.

Both she and Emmett had given their statements, but Emmett had noticed Sergeant Sutherland sizing him up earlier. Impressed that her commander hadn't taken over the task he'd sent her to do, Emmett decided Gavin

Sutherland was tough but fair. He'd want answers, but he'd let Belle do her job to get them.

Belle turned to the dog sleeping on the cart. "I'll walk with you back to your van," she said to Dr. Mazelli before glancing over at Emmett. "I don't like this but an order's an order."

"I'll come with you," Emmett offered. "After you see Justice off, we can go somewhere and have our talk if you feel up to it."

Once they had the dog settled in the back of the big van, Belle rubbed Justice's fur and patted him on his head, her eyes misty. "I'll check on you soon, Justice. I promise."

"I'll call in about an hour or so," the doc said. "I'll give you a full report."

"Gracias," Belle replied, reminding Emmett of her Hispanic heritage. Then she turned back to Emmett. "I live in Fort Greene, but I can take a train home."

The rain came then, fat cold drops that would soon turn into a downpour. They took cover under the trees.

"My place is close by," he said, glancing at the dark sky. "We can talk in private there and…I can keep an eye on you. I'll give you a ride home later."

"I don't think so," she said on a huff of breath, exhaustion tugging at her. "But the sooner we get this over with, the sooner I can go and see Justice. If your place will get me out of this rain, I'll go. But you don't have to worry about taking me home. I'll spend the night at the station so I can be near my partner."

Emmett decided not to argue with Belle Montera.

But he was curious about more than the DNA match the K-9 team had discovered.

Now, he also wanted to know more about this woman and why someone would want to strangle her to death.

TWO

Why had she allowed Emmett to bring her to his apartment? Belle didn't know this man, but she did believe she could trust him. He had a stellar reputation as a high-ranking deputy marshal who served in SOG—the Special Operations Group, a tactical unit, which pretty much gave him carte blanche to do what needed to be done in any situation. He'd certainly done just that tonight. All of that aside, she'd rather be sitting with Justice. But Sarge had reminded her they needed information regarding the DNA match.

"I'll make sure you get back to the station to check on Justice," Emmett said after giving her a towel to dry off. The drizzle outside hadn't soaked them too much. "This was the closest place to talk in private."

He moved around the sparse kitchen, banging some pots and pans before he came over to hand her a glass of sparkling water and two pain pills. "Take these. I'm warming up some soup."

"I don't need soup," she said, exhaustion overtaking her. "I need information."

"Okay, then." Grabbing a soda from the refrigerator, he came back into the den of the well-appointed apartment he'd told her he shared with a lawyer and a doctor.

He'd explained on the quick walk over that he and his roommates never saw each other much so they wouldn't be interrupted here.

"Before I answer *your* questions, do you know why anyone would want to kill you?"

Shaking her head, Belle took a breath, swallowed the pills and drank the water. "No. I mean I've collared a lot of people, but other than shouting at me on the way to the slammer, no one has ever threatened me before. This guy said I'd pay for what I've done." Shrugging, she pushed at her falling hair and tried to readjust her ponytail. "That could be anyone that I've helped put away."

The man sitting across from her studied her for a moment. "So you didn't recognize your attacker?"

"No," she said, a shiver moving down her spine. "He had on dark glasses and a big black hat. His face was full and puffy and he was heavyset. Like a weight lifter, maybe. But he wore a chunky ring—a signet ring. Gold. I remember the gold flashing in my face. Gold etched in black."

Emmett moved closer. "Maybe you can describe both the face and the ring to your forensic artist and then you can run the sketch through the system."

"I'll do that first thing tomorrow," she said, her throat protesting with every word. "Right now, I need to verify the DNA evidence found from a cold-case murder site twenty-years ago when Eddie and Anna McGregor were murdered. You're a match to that DNA evidence, as you know. Can you tell me anything more? Are you familiar with this case?"

Emmett's eyebrows went up. "No, I wasn't familiar with the case, but I did look it up once I was informed that I was a match for the DNA. Am I a suspect?"

"No. We did a thorough background check on you. You were a preteen when the first murder happened, and you lived in another neighborhood. You were the closest match we could find on the public genealogy search site when we reopened the cold case recently. We pulled up this case when we had a similar case a couple of months ago. Double homicide and a child at home at the time. The assailant wore a clown mask with blue hair and gave the child a stuffed toy in a bag."

Filling him in on how twenty years ago Eddie and Anna McGregor were murdered in Bay Ridge, Brooklyn, she said, "Now, we have Alex and Debra Emery shot to death in their home two months ago. Same MO but different neighborhood than the first killings."

"And a child left at the scene?"

"Yes, unharmed but given a stuffed animal in a bag."

Emmett's eyebrows lifted. "And now I'm older and I live close by? So I *could* be considered a suspect in these new murders?"

"Relax, you've been cleared. You were out chasing criminals in the Village on the night of the current murders. We have the exact time and location of your whereabouts."

He let out a sigh of relief. "Of course you would. But someone who's related to me might be involved in both?"

She took a sip of the sparkling water Emmett had given her, the fizz soothing on her throat. "Yes, according to the worn leather watchband found at the cold-case crime scene. It's been tested for a match over the years but no hits. Until now. A relative of yours."

"What happened to the child in the first case?"

"The McGregors had two children, Penelope and Bradley, who were adopted by the lead detective on the case and his wife. Penelope was found at the scene, but outside of the house. She was holding a stuffed animal. A monkey covered in plastic that she said the *bad man* gave her."

Emmett shut his eyes for a moment. Like her, he'd seen the worst of humanity.

"Incidentally, both siblings work in our department now—Penelope, who goes by Penny, is a front-desk receptionist. Bradley is a K-9 detective and works with me in Emergency Services. However, Bradley was a teen when his parents were murdered and also a suspect because of some altercations that took place between his parents and him, but he was cleared. That stigma has stayed with him, though. So this new case—with either the same killer or a possible copycat—hits close to home for our unit."

"I don't remember the original case," he admitted. "And I've been too tied up recently in this undercover sting to even watch the news. But this does sound suspicious on the part of the second murder, especially since you work with the siblings involved in the first case. So you're trying to find a connection?"

"We're trying to find out who was at the scene of the first murder and then we'll see if it ties to the current case, though we have even less evidence to go on from the Emery site."

Emmett rubbed a hand down his face, fatigue coloring his expression. "I can see why this would be a priority for your unit."

"It's been hard on Bradley and Penny. Being at the front desk, she hears everything. It's traumatizing for her."

"I guess it would be terrible for both of them to relive

that kind of trauma," Emmett said. "My gut's telling me this can't be good for whoever this relative is, but I will tell the truth if I can pinpoint anyone for you."

"Tell me about your relatives," she said.

He glanced out the wide windows. The bright lights of the surrounding buildings gave them a great view of the skyline and the Brooklyn Bridge off in the distance. Belle searched his face, thinking he looked honest, but then, people could hide a lot behind a calm demeanor and a handsome face. She knew that firsthand. But she wasn't here to accuse him of withholding information—yet. She had to find out about his family tree so he needed to be honest with her.

Finally, he turned back to her, his stormy eyes pinning her to the comfortable chair by the window. "I only have one close living relative who could be nearby, my father's cousin who's in his sixties now. His grandfather and my mine were brothers. He grew up in Brooklyn, but I have no idea where he is now. Most of our distant relatives are scattered all over the country. That leaves him. But Randall couldn't be a killer."

She let that declaration slide because he'd inadvertently given her a name. "Are you two on good terms?"

"Not really. My dad knew him better since they were closer in age. I saw him every now and then at family gatherings. I think I remember him at the funeral when his grandfather died ten years ago. He's a lot older than me and he stays in and out of trouble and can't seem to get a break in life. I tried to keep up with him, but Randall is a loner."

"Do you have his last known address?"

"No. Last I heard he was living in Pennsylvania in a rural area. He's a recluse and likes living off the grid.

He doesn't trust the law or the government, according to what my dad told me."

Shaking his head, he looked at Belle. "Kind of ironic that you got a hit since Randall would balk at being on a family tree. My mom loved genealogy stuff, though. She found most of her side of the family and had just started on my dad's side but…she suffered a fatal stroke and never recovered. She only lasted a week before she died."

Belle lowered her head and lifted her eyes to him. "I'm so sorry, Emmett. How long ago was that?"

"Couple of years," he said, his tone flat. "My dad passed away five years ago from a heart attack. He'd only been retired a year or so."

"That's tough," Belle said. "Tell me more about your mom's research, if you feel okay about doing that right now. It might help us."

He gave her a slight smile. "She'd be willing to help, I know. She tried to load in every relative she could find— just their names since the site is public. But some of them wanted to send in their information and DNA, too. She was big into that kind of stuff—a hobby of sorts after she retired from working in a Brooklyn retail store for over twenty years." Nodding toward another room, he said, "I have all her findings in a file somewhere in my closet. I wanted to pick up where she left off but can't seem to find the time."

Belle believed him. "So your DNA is in the database because of her efforts?"

He nodded. "My mom had joined up with some of our long-lost relatives to fill in the family tree. I don't know how far she got but I can search her handwritten notes and her computer files. Like I said, most of our living relatives are scattered all over the country."

"Let's get back to the name you mentioned," Belle said, trying to stay focused. But her heart went out to Emmett. He must be all alone now. "Randall, you said?"

Rubbing the back of his neck, Emmett stared at his drink, "Honestly, I haven't seen him in years. He tends to shy away from the law and since my dad was with the NYPD, Randall sure didn't want to hang out with him." After a long pause, he looked over at Belle. "Randall had a hard life, from what my mom told me. His daddy was a mean man who drank himself to death. Randall's mother left when he was a little boy. I don't think he ever got over that. Dad told me once that Randall was always searching for his mom. Breaks my heart, since I had a set of solid, loving parents."

Belle saw the veil of sadness coloring his eyes. "I'm sorry about your parents and I'm sorry your father's cousin had to suffer that way."

"Yeah, me, too." He stood and took her water glass. "I stay busy these days, but my folks are never far from my thoughts. They both had such a strong faith. I wish I could feel the same but doubt seems to follow me around these days."

Belle thought of her own family and was thankful that her parents were still alive and that she had siblings close by, too. They all lived near each other in one of her father's inherited properties in Fort Greene. They fought and argued but they also stuck together, no matter what. Their faith was a big part of their lives. She'd expect no less from Emmett, but if his cousin turned out to be the person of interest in the case, she hoped Emmett would do the right thing.

"That's tough," she said, wanting to know more about

Emmett. "It's nice that you wanted to finish things for your mom, though. So you don't keep in touch with Randall?"

"Not much," Emmett refilled her water glass and then came back with the tomato soup he'd made and handed her the mug along with the fresh water. "He moves around a lot. I know he's been in trouble with the law. My dad tried to watch out for him through the years, but Randall's as stubborn as they come. Likes to do things his way."

"Well, since we can't identify who in your family might be connected, he obviously didn't offer your mother much help. We found the match through a DNA sequencing firm after getting a warrant to do a search. We used a sleuthing geneticist to help us fill in the gaps. But we hit a wall."

"Which means you want me to lead you to Randall, right?"

"Right. We could really use your help in finding him. We need to ask him some questions."

"Sure you do. So, what could be my cousin's DNA was found on this old watchband tagged at the murder scene. That's pretty amazing, but a match is a match."

"It's a fresh lead," she replied, wondering if he'd hedge or try to stall them. Or he could alert his cousin so they'd never be able to question the man. "I can show you the watchband. You might recognize it."

"I could try but remember Randall would have been forty-one years old then. I wasn't exactly into hanging out with him even when we were kids since he's older than me. Barely saw the man except when he'd come by to ask my dad for help or money. The few times I was around him, my father was always present. I don't think he trusted Randall a whole lot."

"He's not in the system, obviously, or we wouldn't be

coming to you for answers. Now that I have his name, I'll do a thorough search. Maybe juvie has something."

"That's a possibility. I can search through my dad's old personal records, too. He would have tried to protect Randall, but he would have also followed the law."

Belle thought about that. "If Randall is involved, he did a good job of hiding all the evidence. The watchband is broken so someone must have lost it at the scene."

"So you think he was at the scene of the original murders and that he might have something to do with this latest double homicide?"

She nodded. "But there's no record of him being a suspect because there were no definitive prints found at the scene. The DNA on the watchband is relevant only to the first murders but if we find a connection, he could be questioned regarding the Emerys, too."

"If he killed the McGregors *and* the Emerys, that would mean he's back in the area. Or was," Emmett said. She could see the wheels turning. After all, he was a US marshal. He knew the drill. "I wonder if my dad knew of the cold case. He had to have heard about it but if Randall was never indicated as a suspect, it could have been off Dad's radar."

Or his well-meaning father could have hidden some evidence? She didn't want to believe that, but it did happen at times. Maybe his father had been at the scene as a police officer? She'd have to check into that.

"So Randall lived in Brooklyn twenty years ago?" she asked to verify before taking a sip of the creamy lukewarm tomato soup. Her throat burned with a hot-pepper fire.

Emmett's eyes went wide while he stood as if debating. "Yes, he did." Giving her a direct stare, he added, "He lived in an apartment above a deli in Bay Ridge."

Belle dropped her pen. "Where the first murders took place."

Emmett sank back against the plaid couch and stared across at her. "This is beginning to sound bad for Randall."

"Do you have any photos of him?" she asked, trying to keep her head while her heart seemed to open a crack or two for this man. He looked so devastated. Emmett might not be close to Randall, but he cared about the family connection. That much was obvious.

"I might. I have my mom's favorite old photo album around here somewhere along with her genealogy files." He got up and went to what must be his bedroom and came back with a thick battered floral album. "My mom kept all kinds of family photos, and I know I saw one in here. One of the few things I saved when I sold my parents' house."

After searching through it, he tugged an old snapshot out of its protective plastic shield. "Here. This was Randall about six years ago at one of our last family get-togethers before both of our fathers passed away."

Belle took the photo and studied the tall wiry man. Randall Gage looked nothing like the man sitting here with her. Where Emmett was all muscle and broad-chested, Randall was skinny but fairly muscular, his face shadowed in a world-weary darkness and his thick hair full of gray streaks.

"Thanks," she said. "We can do a facial recognition on this, I hope."

"Sure. You can scan it on my printer if you want and send it in from here."

Deciding she'd have to trust Emmett, she said, "I need to call this in to Sergeant Sutherland, too."

Emmett nodded and got up to stare out the window.

Could she trust him? He'd mentioned his father keeping notes. Would a good officer have tried to hide evidence to protect a relative?

Belle moved to the kitchen and made the call. But she had to wonder if Emmett would immediately get in touch with his cousin the minute she left.

Stop that, she told herself. Just because she'd had a bad breakup with a security guard who wanted to be a super cop and had told her how to do her job, didn't mean she couldn't trust any other man ever.

Besides, this tall drink of water was off-limits. She'd found Emmett Gage to question him about a murder, not go all gaga over him.

But…

"Belle, are you there?"

"Yes, sir," she replied to Gavin's pointed question. Then she told him what she'd found out. "I'll scan the photo and send it to you and the lab right away. Maybe we'll get a hit on his last known address. Maybe the deputy marshal can help with that, too."

"If he's willing to cooperate, use him. The man is good at his job." Then Gavin added, "When you come by to check on Justice, which I know you will, bring Marshal Gage with you. Now that you've made contact and found a possible lead, I'd like to talk to him."

"Yes, sir." Belle ended the call and went back across the room. "I could use that scanner. Sarge wants to get on this right away and…he wants to speak to you again, too."

Emmett agreed to that. Then he said, "Hey, you mentioned stuffed animals. I found another picture of Randall here. He's very young in this one, but my mom wrote his name and the date on the back of the picture."

Belle stared down at the grainy black-and-white photo. Randall Gage held on tightly to a stuffed animal—a fluffy dog about the size of the two animals found with both of the children in these cases.

"Interesting," she said. But when she saw how crushed Emmett looked when he turned away, she added, "But it doesn't mean anything. We all have stuffed animals and favorite toys as children."

"Randall collected toys and such." Emmett turned around, concern shadowing his face. "I sure hope he'll be cleared. He's got some issues, but murdering someone? A couple with their child close by? I don't know. I can't see it."

"Sometimes, we don't want to see what's right in front of our eyes."

"Spoken like the voice of experience."

Belle followed him into a small office filled with all sorts of electronic equipment. "I'm a pretty positive person and I like to believe the best about people. But I'm also realistic because I've seen the worst in people."

Emmett quickly scanned the photo. "So, you've been disappointed?"

After giving him her phone number so he could message it to her, she said, "Yes. I guess it brings out the bitterness in me."

He put his hand on the black office chair. "Here. You can send it once you receive it."

After emailing the scan to her unit and the lab, she stood and gave Emmett a bold stare. "What's your story, anyway?"

He chuckled, his discomfort evident in the way he

rubbed the back of his neck and moved back into the larger room. "I don't have much of a story. Always wanted to follow in my father's footsteps. Got hooked on being a US marshal after watching *The Fugitive* over and over. Worked hard to get a degree and found a place to land."

"And you landed here in New York? Or are you native like me?"

"I grew up right here in Brooklyn," he said. "This is home. But I travel a lot. Work—that's what I do. I work."

"I should go and check on Justice," she said, thinking they didn't have much left to discuss. He'd been more than willing to cooperate, but he had to be as tired as she was. Emmett Gage seemed like the loner he'd been reputed to be. A self-confirmed bachelor?

"I'm going, too, remember. I mean—I've been summoned. Could wait till morning but your sergeant strikes me as the kind who doesn't like waiting."

Surprised, Belle felt little sensations of awareness dancing up her spine. Little foreign sensations that made a beeline right to her heart. *Don't go there*, she warned.

"I can make it to headquarters by myself but, yes, you might as well talk to him while this is fresh on your mind."

"And I plan on getting you where you need to be in one piece," he told her in a firm tone. "You were injured just a few hours ago and the man who did it got away. I'm escorting you back to the precinct and then home safely, Officer Montera. Got it?"

"Are you always this bossy?"

"When I need to be."

"You do realize that I can be bossy, too."

"Wouldn't want it any other way."

Her cell buzzed, saving her from setting him straight.

"It's Dr. Mazelli." After reading the text, she turned back to Emmett. "Justice is awake. I need to go and see him."

"I'll give you a ride," Emmett said. "My truck is down in the parking garage."

"I'd rather take the subway," Belle said. "I'm staying with Justice tonight so no point in you bringing your truck out. I said I'd be okay."

"I can get you there in about half an hour."

Belle mulled that over. She didn't want to depend on him, but she did want to get to her partner. "Okay. This time we don't have much choice."

Emmett gave her a tight smile. "I have a feeling there'll be more than just this time, Officer Montera."

There they went again. Those warm and fuzzy sensations dancing up and down her spine reminded her that this was such a bad idea, but…Emmett made her feel safe in a way that being confident had never covered. Belle bristled. She *was* confident but this attack had shaken her. Or maybe it was just the pain pills and soup making her all warm and fuzzy.

Which only aggravated her even more because up until tonight she'd always been capable out on her own with Justice.

How could she be a good K-9 officer if she didn't feel confident anymore?

Rubbing her sore neck, Belle knew she'd have to work double time to get her groove back.

And this big, tall, fascinating man could not get in the way of that. She appreciated Emmett's help and his honesty, and while he'd been cleared of being a suspect in this case, she still wondered how far he'd go to protect Randall Gage.

THREE

After Emmett parked across the street from the Brooklyn K-9 Unit building in the only available slot, he followed Belle and took in the precinct building. The limestone building near Owl's Head Park was three stories and had a unique arched facade that made it stand out. The vet's office was right next door in the K-9 training center. Belle had told him he could wait in Sergeant Sutherland's office in the main building. She'd quickly shown him the way to the office and then left in a fast trot to check on her furry partner.

Too antsy to sit, Emmett stood and looked at several pictures of Sergeant Sutherland and his team. Then he noticed a picture of Gavin in a suit with a woman wearing a wedding gown. Obviously, his wife now. The happy couple smiled and held each other while two K-9s stood with what looked like happy grins on their faces.

"That's Stella and Tommy with Officer Brianna Hayes—now Sutherland—and me at our wedding last year," Gavin said from the doorway. "Those two are inseparable unless they're working. Stella's a yellow Lab and she's my wife's partner in bomb detection. They work back in my old precinct in Queens. And Tommy's right here with me—a springer spaniel and also trained in bomb detection."

Emmett turned to face Gavin, noting the man's no-nonsense demeanor had softened when he mentioned his wife and his K-9 partner. Emmett had a feeling this man was inseparable from his wife unless they were working, too. He'd heard how they'd taken down a bomber last July.

"Sounds like a great life."

"I can't complain."

Gavin shook Emmett's hand and offered him a seat. The sergeant's partner, Tommy, gave Emmett a curious look, but Emmett knew not to interact with the dog. Gavin ordered Tommy to stay and the dog settled down beside the big desk.

"So," Gavin began, shuffling files as he went, "Justice is going to be okay. Just groggy. He's off duty for the next couple of days."

"Officer Montera sure is close to her partner," Emmett pointed out. "She wanted to stay here tonight."

Gavin put down the files. "I saw Belle and assured her that she needs to go home tonight." Then he chuckled. "No, I had to make that an order. But yes, we're all close to our partners. They put their lives on the line every day and do it so they can have playtime."

"I need to try that formula for playtime on myself," Emmett admitted. "I understand you have questions for me?"

Gavin nodded. "Belle filled me in. So Randall Gage is your dad's cousin."

"Yes." Emmett repeated the information he'd given Belle earlier. "Since he seems the only likely suspect, I'd like to be involved in tracking him down, if you don't mind."

"Why?" Gavin asked. "You're not planning to tip him off, are you?"

That question riled Emmett, but he knew it had to be asked. "I'm planning on doing my job. If Randall's your man, I want to be there when you take him in. I don't want him to do anything stupid and get himself killed."

"Fair enough," Gavin replied, his dark eyes as blank as an empty pistol. "You might keep an eye on Officer Montera, too."

"Excuse me?"

"Someone tried to kill one of my officers tonight. You were there. You want in on this investigation, then you watch my officer's back, got it? Because Belle will be front and center on this case."

Emmett lifted his head. "Got it. Watch and stay out of the way unless needed. I can observe and offer my assistance but not overstep, right?"

Gavin gave him an appreciative stare. "Exactly."

They talked a bit more, Emmett giving Gavin as much information on his cousin as he could remember. "If he's back in the area, I'll find him and bring him in myself," he assured Gavin.

A knock at the open door caused both of them to glance around. "Nate?" Gavin motioned the muscular blond-haired man in. "Marshal Emmett Gage, meet K-9 Officer Nate Slater. He's a detective and his partner, Murphy, is cross-trained to deal with anything."

Emmett stood and shook the officer's hand, prepared to leave. "I'm cross-trained myself. Give Murphy my best."

Nate's blue eyes widened. "I'll do that. Actually, I need to ask you a question, Marshal Gage."

"Sure," Emmett said, his gut telling him this had to be about the McGregor case.

"Does your cousin Randall happen to have a deep baritone voice?"

Emmett thought about the last time he'd talked to Randall. He had to tell the truth. "He does but it's grainy now from years of smoking. But yes, I'd say his voice is deep."

"Thanks," Nate said, his expression turning grim. "That may be of help with the most recent case."

"Is he a suspect in the second murders?" Emmett asked, his gut now burning.

"We don't know yet," Nate admitted. "Too early to tell." He thanked Emmett and left. Meaning, he didn't want to reveal too much too soon.

"Okay, we have enough for now," Gavin finally said. "I'd advise you let us work on this as much as possible while you do your job, but I'll keep you informed and you can ride along with Belle as needed. If push comes to shove, you can move in with us."

"Deal." Emmett liked Gavin's straight talk.

Gavin stood. "I'll show you the way to the vet's office."

"I'll escort Officer Montera home," Emmett said, making it clear he wouldn't back down.

"Thank you." Gavin pointed to the hallway and then turned to leave. "And thanks for your cooperation."

Emmett nodded and then Gavin led him to the vet's office.

He found Belle sitting by a table where Justice lay sleeping, her hand holding the big dog's paw. Studying her from the door, Emmett took in her straight dark brown hair and her olive skin. She was a beautiful woman and a tough one at that. From here, he could see the bruises and marks on her slender neck.

His blood boiled. He not only planned to help her find his cousin. He planned to help her track down the person who'd done this to her, too. Emmett knew the kind. If this guy had a vendetta, he'd keep coming. Sure, she was trained in one of the toughest jobs in the city but… still…she was in danger and she'd have to watch her back.

But Emmett would have her six, whether she wanted him to or not. That's just the way things had to be right now since the attacker could come back for both of them.

And meantime, he'd work with Belle and the Brooklyn K-9 Unit to find Randall. He only hoped his cousin wouldn't be given a guilty charge before he had a chance to be exonerated. Maybe Randall had an alibi or maybe he could explain why his watchband had become evidence toward a double homicide.

Emmett had to know the truth, either way. He'd start by searching his father's old files.

Belle glanced up and saw him at the door. Taking a last look at Justice, she leaned down and whispered in the big dog's ear, her hand brushing his silky coat.

Emmett's heart did a funny little twist after seeing the sweet gesture. There was something about this strong, tough woman that made him appreciate her and also want to protect her. He knew she'd balk at the protection. She had been trained in all things tactical, so she didn't need a hero to come to her rescue. He'd just watch over her without making a big deal of it.

He had to. He was all in now.

Belle glanced back at Justice one more time. She really didn't like leaving him. "We're rarely apart," she said to Emmett as he led her out of the building. "I should stay in case he wakes up."

"Your sergeant told me he ordered you to go home and rest and to stay home tomorrow, too. You need to take it easy. You'll be sore in the morning."

She didn't answer but she didn't bolt, either. It figured that Gavin would alert Emmett that he'd ordered her to go home. They'd ganged up on her along with Gina Mazelli and a couple of her coworkers.

Once the word was out about what had happened, several members of their unit had come by the precinct to check on both Belle and Justice. Her friend Vivienne Armstrong and her K-9 partner, Hank, a border collie, happened to be running through some training sets when they'd brought Justice in. Vivienne had sat with Belle while she'd talked to Justice and lulled him back to sleep.

"He'll be fine, Belle. I know it's scary to see him so still and out of it, but the doc knows her stuff."

Vivienne's reassurances had helped but this day seemed to be dragging on and on. And now, she had a big US marshal shadowing her. She should have been appreciative but instead she felt defeated.

"I'm too tired to make a big deal out of this," she admitted as they headed toward Emmett's truck. "But you don't have to take me home. I can take the subway."

She stepped out ahead of him and checked the street. In the next instant, a motorcycle roared to life and came screeching toward Belle. She looked up, the bike's bright headlight blinding her and freezing her to the asphalt.

Then she felt strong hands wrapping around her waist and lifting her into the air. Emmett grabbed her and pulled her back, both of them toppling over onto the sidewalk in the split second just before the biker flew by. Emmett managed to take the brunt of the fall but Belle landed across his chest, her eyes crashing with his as they stared at each other.

Her heart beat in triple time and she thought she might pass out again but Belle felt the pull of his gaze.

"Are you all right?" he asked as he quickly sat up and helped her do the same. Belle noticed the spicy scent of his aftershave and reminded herself that she was tired and someone had tried to do her in twice tonight. Her mind was playing tricks on her in too many ways to analyze right now.

"Yes," she said, out of breath. "Did that guy try to run me down?"

"I think so," Emmett replied, the sound of the bike roaring off in the distance. "I didn't have time to get a good look. All I saw was a blur of man and machine."

"I didn't see anything," Belle said, wondering if she truly would be out of commission for a few days since her mind didn't seem to be functioning. "You saved my life again, Emmett. I'm pretty sure that's the same man who attacked me in the park. Remember, I heard a bike cranking before I was attacked and then right after he ran away."

"Yeah, well, I'm just glad I was here to help and witness this. Makes sense it's the same person. We need to report this to Sergeant Sutherland."

Belle shook her head. "I'll call him from your truck. The guy on that bike is long gone, I'm beat and every muscle in my body aches. I can't bring myself to file another report tonight. I want to go home but I don't know what I'll do without Justice. He's always by my side. Now I have to worry about him getting hurt."

"Hey, you're still tough and so is Justice," Emmett said. "You'll both be fine soon enough. But you shouldn't be alone. Too dangerous."

"I live in a building that my parents own," she explained. "My grandparents bought up apartment buildings in Fort Greene way back in the seventies and my dad took over when they moved to a retirement home. He now owns several rentals. We all live in one building. I have a younger brother and two younger sisters who pound on my apartment door day and night. I'm never alone, trust me."

"All right." Emmett checked her over, his piercing glances giving her an up close and personal opportunity to look him over, too. Again, a heated awareness covered her. His winded whisper only added to that. "Are you sure you don't need a doctor? Maybe you should talk to Gavin?"

Suddenly feeling smothered and all too aware that someone wanted to do her harm, she shook her head. "I want to get out of here. Now."

Emmett gave her a concerned stare. "Okay."

She was close to a crash and burn, and she didn't want it to happen in front of her team or her sergeant. Maybe Emmett had figured that out.

"Let's go," he said, guiding her to his truck. Once he had her inside, he leaned against the passenger-side door and said, "You know, you're kind of exciting to be around, Officer Montera."

"Yeah, I'm just a barrel of laughs," she retorted on a shaky voice. "Except someone doesn't think I'm much fun."

"*I* think you can be," he said, "when you're not being chased by someone out to do you in."

Once she'd called Gavin to give him the latest, Belle didn't say much on the drive to Fort Greene. Instead, she stared out at the buildings along the Brooklyn–Queens

Expressway just before they passed Sunset Park. She could barely hold her eyes open, but she managed to direct Emmett to her apartment off Lafayette Avenue. Emmett pulled up to the curb in front of the multi-level brick building with white trim and white wrought iron mini-balconies. The foursquare looked like a big row house, but right now it looked like home. Belle was ready to go to sleep in the safety of that home.

"I'm on the bottom floor because of Justice needing a dog run," she said, pointing to a corner apartment of the three-story apartment building. "We have a nice little yard out back with a sturdy fence."

"I'm walking you to your door."

He didn't let her say no. Now she'd have to explain to her parents. Maybe they could sneak by the main entryway to the stairs without any family drama. Her family worried that she hadn't dated since her last fiasco of a boyfriend. Hard to explain that her line of work didn't allow for any fun late nights or online dating sites.

But if her sisters got a glance of Emmett Gage, they'd get the wrong impression. Then she'd have to give her family the real reason for his being there.

"I can make it from here," she said when they entered the stoop and she keyed in the door code.

Emmett kept standing there. "I'd like to come inside."

"You're annoying."

"I hear that a lot."

"I'm fine, really," she said as they went through the vestibule. A long central hallway ran the length of the bottom floor. The apartments on the other side of hers were used for family members passing through and storage. The rest of the building was her family's two-story home, where she hung out a lot. Her siblings slept on the third floor.

Emmett filled the hallway with his presence. "I'm right behind you, really."

She made it to her door and tried to get the key in the lock. Emmett took it and managed to unlock the door, adding to her humility.

But when he opened it, he stumbled on a yellow mailing envelope, his gaze moving from that to Belle.

"Were you expecting mail?"

"Not shoved underneath my door, no." Glancing around, she added, "How did someone get in here?"

"We can figure that out later. Right now we need to find out what this is," he said. "Don't touch it yet."

Belle shifted around the letter-sized envelope. Emmett picked it up with a tissue he'd found in the box on the counter and Belle found latex gloves so she could open it.

The handwritten scribbles said it all.

I intend to finish what I started. You ruined my life. I intend to ruin yours. Maybe I'll find one of your sisters next.

Belle's heart accelerated as her gaze met Emmett's. Then her mind went wild with speculations. Was this just an idle threat or was her attacker going to come after her family, too?

FOUR

"That's a *definite* threat," Emmett said, his eyes scanning the dark street and the trees around the building. "It had to have come from your attacker but when did he leave it here? We'll brush for prints and you should alert your sergeant."

"I'll report it now and talk to Gavin tomorrow," she said. "I'm thinking we won't find any prints since he slipped it through the door. First, I want to check on my family."

She stopped in the hallway. "I don't want to alarm them but I do need to beef up security and alert them on what's going on. This man is dangerous. I feared that they'd be targeted because of me and now it's happening."

"Okay. *I'll* call it in and report we're together and things are under control," Emmett replied. "You're right. Your family needs to be aware."

Belle searched the bottom floor but found nothing unusual while he made the call. Quick and efficient and in charge, Emmett handled everything with a strength she wished she had.

Thankful that he was with her, she motioned toward the entryway stairs. "My parents and my brother and sisters live up here. My dad converted these two floors into one unit."

Emmett followed her up the stairs. "The door looks solid. No sign of a break-in."

"I have a key. We need to check on my family." Belle silently unlocked the door. Darkness greeted them. "They should all be in bed by now. Wait here."

Emmett took in the apartment. Average in size but clean and neat with a long narrow hallway toward the back with stairs up to the next floor. Her family had obviously taken over this whole foursquare and turned it into a big family unit.

After she'd done a room check, Belle tiptoed back. They were almost out the door when Emmett heard footsteps.

"Belle?"

"Cara, what are you doing up?"

From what he could tell in the muted darkness, the girl was in her teens and looked like a petite version of Belle but her dark hair was longer. "I heard a noise."

"Just now, you mean?" Belle asked, urgency in her question. "Did you hear anyone coming in earlier?"

"*Sí*. I was reading and I heard you open the door." The girl's eyes widened when she noticed Emmett. "But Joaquin came home about an hour ago. Is something wrong? Your voice sounds funny."

Giving Emmett a warning glance, Belle replied, "I strained my throat earlier when we got into a scuffle with a perp. I'll be fine. Sorry I woke you up. I was just checking since I had to work late." Then she glanced around. "Was our brother okay?"

Cara bobbed her head. "Snarly, as usual, and sneaking in. I didn't rat him out, though."

Belle didn't comment. Emmett wondered if their brother had seen someone or had even taken the envelope from someone in front of the building and left it under her door.

The girl motioned to the kitchen. "We have leftover chicken spaghetti in the fridge."

"I'm not hungry," Belle said on a low note. "You should go back to bed."

Cara rubbed her eyes and crossed her arms over her big nightshirt before sending Emmett a direct stare. "Who is he?"

Emmett had to smile at that blunt question. "I'm Emmett, a friend of your sister's."

Cara's eyes widened as she came fully awake. "A friend? Belle, you didn't tell us you were dating again."

"I'm not," Belle said on a slightly agitated sigh. "We're not. It's not that way. We had a business meeting."

Her sister's eye roll was classic. "Right. Nice to meet you, Emmett. I'm going back to bed now."

Belle waited until her sister was back in her room. "Sorry about that."

"She's something, huh?"

"You could say that. Her twin is not quite as forthcoming. Anita is quiet and loves to read. Cara is more of a girlie girl with an attitude. Sweet sixteen and going on thirty."

They moved back down to her apartment. Emmett could tell she was embarrassed by the way she refused to look at him and then started explaining. "I was in a serious relationship for a couple of years, but it ended badly. Now they all hold their breaths hoping I'll find someone new."

Emmett followed her inside the apartment and let that tidbit settle over him. "Have you been dating again?"

Giving him a stern stare, she said, "Is that really any of your business?"

"Nope. Just curious."

He had to watch himself around this one. She was pretty and smart and tough. No flirting. No anything but finding out the truth about his cousin possibly being a murderer and trying to protect Belle. Moving with her around the combined kitchen and dining area that flowed into a tiny den, he waited when she turned on the lights and checked the bedroom and bath, all the while reminding himself that he had rules about dating any woman in law enforcement and apparently she had her own set of rules.

"All clear," she said. "Normally, Justice makes the rounds with me. I miss him."

Safe subject. "How did you and Justice become partners?"

She smiled and pushed at her messy bun. "I joined Emergency Services a little over a year ago, after being on another K-9 team with the NYPD for two years. My K-9 partner, Rocket, stayed with that unit after a trainer moved up the ranks. Justice had finished his initial training when he became my partner. We trained in Emergency Services together and he's been by my side almost every day since training."

"You two obviously make a good team," Emmett said. Then he looked her over. "How you feeling?"

"I'll feel better after a hot shower and more pain pills. And sleep."

"That's my cue to leave." He pointed to the dead bolt and the chain locks. "Lock up tight and fill in your sergeant a little more tomorrow."

"I will. I'll take this straight to the lab to be analyzed and then I'm going to search mug shots and old case files."

Emmett knew she'd do it, too. "I'll check with you tomorrow and report anything else I can find on Randall."

"Thanks." She looked down at the floor and then back up to him. "It was nice to meet you, Emmett." Then she let out a nervous little laugh. "Really nice, considering."

He smiled at that. "We dodged a bullet, literally. That guy's aim was seriously off."

"Which means at least he's not a professional."

"Nowhere near." He studied her for a moment. "I'm thinking he's someone you put away and now he's back and out for revenge. Report the motorcycle incident, too. Like you mentioned, he must have used that to get away at the park earlier."

"I don't know how he got access to this building," she said, thinking of how she'd always gone to a lot of trouble to make sure her family's home was secure.

"He might have slipped in when someone from your family opened the main door. Or it could have been a person your family knows and trusts."

"I'll go over my cases and I'll talk to my parents," she said. "I certainly never expected this when I made plans to meet with you."

"Me, either."

"Good night," she said. "I'll talk to you soon."

Emmett left but he checked around the building before he got back in his truck. That man tonight had been serious. He would have killed Belle if Emmett hadn't come along in the park, and he'd come to the police station and waited for her to exit. Now her attacker had made a bold move by coming to her home to leave a threat.

Emmett would urge Gavin to put a watch on this place in case the intruder returned.

Emmett said a prayer of thanks and drove back to his

apartment. Unable to sleep, he pulled out his mother's genealogy files and tried to decipher the many ways to find a family member and narrow down the odds of a match. Any one of the several distant relatives he had on his father's side could also be a match, but none of them lived in the state of New York.

He'd need to find Randall and try to get some fresh DNA to back up the K-9 Unit's claims. But in his gut, he figured Randall looked pretty good for the cold-case murder.

Randall, who'd been abandoned by his mother and abused by his father, ultimately had suffered a lot of setbacks in life. What would have motivated him to kill the couple, though? Had he known them? And had he also killed little Lucy Emery's parents or was that the work of a copycat?

Just a few of the many questions he'd have to ask Randall if he ever found him.

The next morning, Belle looked up from the laptop on her desk. She'd been going through mug shots for what seemed like hours, but now she saw Emmett walking toward her with two cups from her favorite coffee shop.

"Here," he said, greeting her with a weary smile. He also offered her a small white paper bag, then pulled out a bagel and held it. "I brought you an apple Danish, too. Softer on your throat than a bagel."

"Thanks, that was thoughtful." Ignoring all the warning bells in her head, she took a long sip of the coffee and grimaced when it hit her sore throat.

"Still tender?" he asked, examining the red welts over her collar.

"Yes. Sore and bruised and uncomfortable, but I told my family I might have a stalker. I also asked Sarge to put a patrol on our apartment building and then came here and updated him and the team on everything that happened after we left the park. I talked him into letting me come in today to go through mug shots."

"Wore him down?"

"Something like that." Tapping her fingers on the desk, she said, "My parents are concerned, of course. But my Papá has a whole system of people who watch out for our neighborhood. Not vigilantes but a strong watch, all the same. *Familia* is very important to him."

Her parents didn't like her line of work, so the stalker talk had not gone over well, but she'd assured them she was okay and as long as they were careful, they should be safe. Papá said he'd inform the neighbors. He'd put citizen watchers on every corner.

"As long as you don't take the law into your own hands," she'd warned. Her father respected the NYPD, so he knew the rules.

"How's Justice?" Emmett asked now while he tore into the giant bagel.

"I saw him first thing," she said, keeping her voice low because it hurt to try to talk on an even keel. "He's much better. We had some playtime, but Doc suggested I pamper him for a couple of days. Since Sarge told me to take it easy, Justice and I will hang out in the training arena later and do some low-key practice runs. I should be able to take him home tonight."

"That sounds like a good plan."

"But first, I'd like to see if I can ID the man from last night."

Belle broke off a piece of the fluffy Danish and chewed it. Then she took a swallow of the herbal tea with honey and lemon her friend and coworker Lani Jameson had made for her. "I need a caffeine boost so I'll drink the coffee, too," she told Emmett since he'd gone out of his way to bring it to her.

After explaining that she was drinking the tea to soothe her throat, she went on to tell him about the female K-9 officer who'd taken Belle under her wing when Belle had first started here.

"Lani likes to nurture everyone. She's married to Noah Jameson, the chief at the NYC K-9 Command Unit in Queens. Her partner is Snapper, the German shepherd that worked with Chief Jordan Jameson. Sadly, he was murdered last year and Snapper went missing for a while."

Emmett rubbed a finger on his chin. "I remember that—a big shake-up and such a senseless murder."

"Yes. I worked in another unit but…it shook up the whole NYPD."

"Glad they found the killer." Emmett finished his bagel. "So what's the status on *your* attacker?"

She pointed to the screen. "I've met with the forensic artist and based on the sketch and the man's build, I'm trying to narrow things down while the lab works on getting a facial match."

"Any luck yet?"

"No, but the techs are going over the epidermis scrapings and hair follicles they found on my clothes so we should get something one way or another. The artist sketched the ring, too. Our techie, Esme Chang, offered to do some research on that, but it might be nothing." Shaking her head, she added, "I have nothing to go on for the bike. But Sarge has people looking for any motorcycles in this area. A long shot."

He sat next to her and ran a hand down his jawline, giving her a chance to see him in the light of day. Handsome but looking kind of world-weary. But those eyes.

Stormy gray and so serious. He was a nice-looking man. Today, he wore a navy polo shirt with a Justice Department emblem on the top left side and khaki pants, his badge on a black lanyard around his neck.

"Did you get any sleep?" she asked to take her mind off the way he seemed to stare right through her.

"Not much." He took a sip of his coffee. "How 'bout you?"

She shook her head. "Too much information jarring my tired brain and too many images of that man with his meaty hands around my throat."

"It'll take time to get over that, but you're tough." He glanced at her neck. "I'll do my best to track Randall down, online, finding his last known address and work records, and through my local sources in this area, and I'll continue to stay on the alert regarding your attacker, but…I can only do so much."

Surprised, Belle frowned at him. "Hey, I can fight my own battles, but thanks. Besides, we both need to locate your cousin."

Emmett nodded in greeting to some officers moving around. They probably all knew who he was since Belle had given a thorough report in this morning's briefing, her voice still hoarse. He seemed to take the scrutiny with ease. Nothing seemed to ruffle this man.

Glancing back at her, he said, "I went through some of my mom's files and found out I have several cousins all over the state of New York but they're only listed on her tree so their information could be private and the rules on how law enforcement can obtain information seem to change frequently. But we could get more warrants. This might turn out to be someone besides Randall."

"But still someone you're related to."

He shot her a wry smile. "Yep. I guess we can't all be in law enforcement."

Belle could see he was worried. "I'm sorry we had to drag you into this, Emmett. If you don't want to be part of the search, I'd understand."

"I do want in on the search," he replied. "If Randall is guilty, I'll be the first to handcuff him. But I'd like to keep him alive and I'd like to obtain DNA from him to verify our suspicions."

"We'll do our best. That's why we need to find him."

Emmett eyed the half of her Danish she hadn't eaten.

"Are you still hungry?" she asked through a grin.

"I guess I am," he replied. "I usually cook bacon and eggs but left in a hurry to get here."

She stopped her search long enough to offer him the rest of the half-eaten Danish. "I guess I wasn't too hungry but thanks."

Emmett gave her a grateful smile.

Then she turned back to the screen. "Hey, wait." Putting down her food, she pointed to a mug shot. "I think this is him, Emmett."

Emmett studied the photo and the information, then read it out loud. "Lance Johnson. Twenty-eight years old. Repeat offender." He read off the rap sheet and then halted. "Domestic abuse." He looked at Belle. "Well now, that makes sense."

"I remember him now," she said, ignoring the shiver that slipped down her spine. "Big and hefty and a bully. I caught him attacking a woman over a year ago in the very park we were in last night. One of my first collars and Justice was there to help take him down."

"That would explain why he tranquilized your partner."

Belle studied the mug shot. "He's changed some. More beefed up. He must have worked out in prison."

"I got a good look at him but couldn't make out his face. I do remember he was hefty." Emmett sat up and scanned the photo. "Are you sure he's your assailant?"

"Oh, yeah. The woman he attacked that night was his ex-girlfriend. He'd beaten her before, and she'd left him but he tracked her down. She called 911 and I was in the area and first on the scene. She testified against him, and the prosecution also brought out that his ex-wife had filed abuse charges against him and then dropped them."

Shrugging, she said, "But the judge ruled that as inadmissible since the ex-wife had dropped the charges. That incident happened before the new state law allowing prosecutors to go forward on those types of charges even if the victim didn't press charges."

She hit print on the file and then whirled her chair around. "It was ruled as a misdemeanor, and he did go to prison but the sentencing was not long enough in my opinion. Domestic abuse cases can swing both ways, depending on probable cause and the strength of the evidence and testimonies. Only a year in jail, a fine and then probation. Which I'm thinking he's probably already broken."

"We need to check with his probation officer."

"On it," Belle replied to Emmett's suggestion. "Let me go and talk to Sarge so he'll reconsider making me stay by my desk. If we can get this suspect off my back, I'll have more time to help you search for your cousin."

Emmett wouldn't mind spending more time with her, but their duties had to come first. He needed to remember that and keep his head in the game.

FIVE

Two hours later, Belle and Emmett walked into a small office inside the Kings County courthouse. They needed to talk to Johnson's probation officer, a man named Sam Blain.

After they explained why they were there, Sam Blain sank back in a rickety office chair, his face dour and his eyes bloodshot.

Rubbing his bald head, he grunted. "Lance Johnson hasn't checked in the last two weeks and I couldn't find him at his last known address. I've alerted the proper authorities and filed a violation with the court. Since no one can locate the man, I had no choice."

"Can we have his last known address?" Belle asked, her mind on getting this done. "I really need to question him."

"Humph. You and me both, lady." Sam grunted again and pulled out Lance Johnson's file. "He's one angry man. Didn't like jail and keeps saying he was framed. Started griping the first week he reported to me and now it's three weeks in and he's a no-show. I wouldn't put it past him to go after everyone involved in this case. If he did attack you, he might try to find all of his exes, too. Could get ugly."

"We'll alert them," Emmett replied, giving Belle a knowing glance. "Has he made any threat toward anyone that you're aware of?"

"That boy makes threats toward anybody who looks at him sideways. I see jail again in his future regardless. Hotheaded and desperate, not willing to follow the program."

They left and headed to the address he'd jotted down on a sticky note. It was located in Canarsie, on the fourth floor of a rundown apartment building over a dry-cleaning business.

Once they cleared the crumbling stairs up, the heat inside the dank, narrow hallways made the air stifling, the smell of this morning's bacon still lingering in the air. Belle twisted the collar of her uniform, her raw skin burning once they'd climbed to the fourth floor. "This should be the place."

She knocked loudly on the flimsy door.

No answer.

But a couple of dogs down the way started barking in response to the knocks.

Emmett knocked this time and called out, "Lance Johnson."

Other doors creaked open as people peeked out to see what the ruckus was and after seeing uniforms, slammed their doors shut.

"I have a feeling our man's not at home," Emmett said on a whisper.

"Let's go to the lobby and see if we can find the super or a manager."

They trekked back down to the shoebox lobby that held mailboxes and a small office.

Belle walked into the office. "NYPD," she announced. "Anyone here?"

They heard shuffling and a bald-headed man wearing a faded green shirt and paint-splattered black pants came out of a back room carrying a Chinese takeout box.

Giving them a worried stare, the man put down the container. "Sorry, I'm on break."

"This won't take long," Belle said, flashing her credentials. After introducing herself and Emmett, she asked, "What's your name?"

The man's brow furrowed up. "Albert Stein." Eying his lunch, he shifted on his feet. "What do you need, Officer?"

She pulled out her phone and showed Albert Johnson's mug shot. "We're looking for Lance Johnson, fourth floor, apartment 410."

The grumpy man eyed the photo and moved some papers around before he dropped his lunch on the counter, his expression going blank. "Yeah, I know him. Ain't seen him in a week or so and he owes me rent. He won't be living here much longer if he doesn't pay up."

Belle noted the man's downcast eyes. What was he hiding? "He's late on the rent?"

"Yep, he's been here a month now and next month's rent has been due for a week." He waved his hand up. "Not the best tenant I've ever had."

Belle saw a flash of gold on the man's hand.

He wore a gold signet ring rimmed in black.

Giving Emmett a warning stare, she went on. "So you don't have any idea where we can find Mr. Johnson?"

"Nope. Like I said, he owes me money. But good riddance. The man is always fighting with somebody about something, you know what I mean?"

"Yeah, we know," Emmett replied on a droll note. "We might be back with a search warrant. He could be in a whole lot of trouble."

Albert plopped down on a rickety chair. "I'm the landlord and maintenance man here and I'm telling you, I got nothing. No information on that troublemaker."

Belle motioned to his left hand. "That's an interesting ring you got there. Where did you get it?"

The man dropped his food and stood up. "Look, I answered your questions about Johnson. Where I shop is none of your business. Now can I please eat my General Tso's chicken before it congeals?"

"Sure, you enjoy your lunch," Emmett said. "If you spot Johnson, give my friend here a call, okay?"

Belle handed him a card. "It's important."

"It always is," Albert said, his chopsticks ready. "If he's in trouble with the law, he's outta here."

After they were headed back to her SUV, Belle glanced over at Emmett. "That's the ring my attacker wore. I know it is. Gold with an onyx rim. Like a crest."

Surprised, he asked, "Do you think Albert is your man?"

"No. I matched the attacker to the mug shot we found. It's Lance Johnson. But I think Albert knows more than he's letting on."

Checking traffic, she peeled out of the parking space they'd found down the street. "I'll keep an eye on Albert while I try to find out more about that ring. Why would he and my attacker both be wearing the same kind of unique ring, anyway?"

Emmett ended his phone call and turned back to watch Belle go through some paces with Justice in the indoor training arena. He'd had to get special permission from the chief US marshal of the East New York district to help Belle find his cousin. He couldn't shirk his own duties too long. Due to his Special Operations status, he could get called to travel and he'd have to leave at a minute's notice.

All the more reason to get this done and soon. Emmett tended to get antsy when he was out chasing bad guys. Watching Belle now, he decided this woman made him antsy, too. It had been a while since he'd even tried to date anyone. He needed to remember his rules and stick to his standards. Dating was tough enough without adding in law enforcement on both sides. Watching his mother fret and worry when he was growing up, he'd told himself time and again he didn't want to put anyone through that and most of the women he'd dated didn't appreciate him being absent on a regular basis.

This woman lived and breathed the danger. She got what his job entailed. He couldn't deny she'd gotten to him, but he had to stick to the job of finding bad guys.

"That's a good boy," Belle told Justice as the big dog jumped over a hurdle and climbed up a ladder. Belle had explained how Justice only got one meal a day—at dinner, and he rarely got treats. Instead, these dogs were rewarded with playtime. Emmett was learning more and more about the Brooklyn K-9 Unit as he moved through the corridors of the main building and the training areas.

Dedicated and hardworking. Determined, too, from the way Belle and Justice both tried to bounce back from their ordeal. These officers and their K-9 partners were together almost 24/7. He felt like a third-wheel.

Meantime, he'd put out some feelers regarding his wayward cousin. Nothing on that yet, but he held out hope that Randall would turn up in the old stomping grounds around Brooklyn.

After he left here, he'd try to find his dad's files. He'd have to go to the storage unit he'd rented to hold some of the things he'd kept from his parents' house.

"What are you looking so serious about?" Belle asked after she and Justice were done.

"My old home," he admitted. "I sold it a year after my mom passed. Since I travel a lot, I needed something smaller and with less maintenance. The roommate situation came up and I jumped on the apartment in Dumbo. But I did save a few things. I rented a storage unit not far from where we used to live. I'm going there later on to see if I can find any of my dad's files and notebooks."

"So there might be information on Randall there?"

"I don't know. My dad would have followed the law, but like me, he would have tried to do his best by Randall, too. I know he kept some personal files at home, and he took meticulous notes on all of his cases."

"I could go with you and help," she offered. "Justice is clear to go, and he can stand guard. An easy assignment."

Emmett laughed when Justice's ears perked up. "I think he likes that idea but as long as you don't overdo it. I'll buy dinner."

"I'm starving," she said. "Let me get cleaned up."

They started walking toward the locker room.

"Hey, what did you find on our friend Albert Stein?"

"Nothing yet," she said. "Looks like he has a clean record but…I got the impression he could be shifty. You know how you get a certain vibe?"

"Yep, part of the job. Instincts kick in. I felt the same way."

"I'll be back in a few," she said. "C'mon, Justice. You get to go home with me tonight."

Justice woofed and danced around. The canine seemed to be on the mend.

Emmett settled into a chair in an anteroom and watched as officers and their partners returned for the shift change.

A tall officer with auburn brown hair walked by, a sleek Malinois at his side. The man glanced at Emmett and kept walking but then he turned and came back.

"Hey," Emmett said when the officer stepped into the room. Noticing the name on the officer badge, he added, "Officer McGregor."

"Bradley. And this is my partner, King."

"Long day?" Emmett said, knowing why Bradley McGregor had come back around.

"You could say that. You know who I am, right?"

"Yep, and I'm guessing you know who I am?"

"Right." Bradley stood there with his hands by his sides. "I not sure what to say to you."

"Say what's on your mind," Emmett suggested. "Or I can say it for you. My cousin might have murdered your parents twenty years ago." He saw a flash of pain in Bradley's eyes. "I'm truly sorry for what you and your sister have been through."

Bradley sank down on the chair across from him and told his K-9 partner, King, to stay. The dog got comfortable by his boots.

"Yeah," Bradley said. "I'm not judging, and I won't jump to conclusions. I hope we can both get some answers."

"That's why I'm hanging around," Emmett said. "I've already told Officer Montera I'll be the first to bring Randall in for questioning. That's part of my job, same as yours. But I want this to be handled in a fair way, too. He's innocent until proven guilty."

"I agree," Bradley said. "I know how it feels to be accused of something you didn't do."

Emmet could understand that. He knew that Bradley McGregor, as a teenager who hadn't gotten along with his parents, had been the prime suspect in their murders until he'd finally been cleared. But the suspicion had lingered in public perception. Emmett had heard enough of those kinds of stories from his dad. "I'll find my cousin and we'll get to the truth so you and your sister can find some closure, okay?"

Bradley stood and offered Emmett his hand. "Okay. Thanks."

"You got it." Emmett watched Bradley and King head toward the locker room. He needed to keep digging. These people wanted answers and so did he.

Belle finished her salad and glanced over at Emmett. "You've been kind of quiet. Is all of this catching up with you?"

Emmett pushed his plate back, his hamburger steak finished. Belle had recommended a diner near the precinct and they'd scooted in for a bite before they headed for the storage unit. Justice sat at her feet. He'd had his dinner earlier after they'd finished their workout and he'd had playtime with his favorite hamburger-shaped squeaky toy.

"I talked to Bradley McGregor while I was waiting for you earlier," he said, his tone quiet. "He saw me and stopped in. I think he wanted to check me out and see if he could trust me."

Belle gave him a sympathetic stare. "The whole team

is on this case and…it's not easy. We knew bringing you in would be awkward, but you have every right as an officer of the law to want to find your cousin."

"But it could be considered a conflict of interest. I don't want anyone to resent me being involved."

Belle couldn't help it. She liked this man. He was the real deal and he put the law above everything else, just as they all did. She wasn't ready to drop her guard yet. "Look, people will talk, but Sarge vouched for you and I've reassured people that you want to find Randall and question him. That's the first step. We'll worry about who we offend later. We don't know much now. We need Randall's DNA to know if he's a match for the particle found on that broken watchband."

Her cell buzzed and she held up a finger. "It's our tech guru, Eden Chang.

"Hey, Eden. Do you have news on the DNA lifted from my clothes and fingernails?"

"Yep," Eden said. "I'm reporting for the crime scene techs since we compared notes. DNA matches Lance Johnson. Same with the envelope he left under your door. No prints on the envelope but one or two prints on the actual paper. He's your man. We got facial recognition from the sketch to back it up. Sarge put out a BOLO on him. So be aware."

Breathing a sigh of relief, Belle asked, "What about the ring?"

Eden told her that the ring Belle had described could be a knockoff of an expensive gold signet ring.

"I'm guessing he either stole it or he bought it on the cheap from a costume jewelry store," Eden said. "If he'd stolen it, why would he wear it? He'd hock it right away. Until we have the ring, we can't really say. But we can rule out it being any type of insignia for an organization or club. I didn't find any matches on that and didn't find anything on that type of ring missing or stolen recently."

"Thank you," Belle said. Then she ended the call and reported back to Emmett. "So…now we need to locate Lance Johnson *and* your cousin."

"Let's get to the storage unit," Emmett suggested after he tossed two twenties on the table. "We'll start there, and I can run some more detailed checks when I get home, too. The sooner we find Randall, the sooner we can end this one way or another."

"Meantime, I've asked for the NYPD's assistance guarding my apartment building," Belle said. "I don't need Johnson snooping around there and messing with my family." Or worse, hurting one of them.

SIX

Belle watched while Emmett went through heavy plastic storage bins and cardboard boxes marked to show their content. Some of the containers came with the storage closet and some he'd obviously brought here himself. But this wasn't much stuff and certainly didn't give her a clue as to who he really was.

But then, like most law enforcement people, he lived for his work and probably liked to keep to himself. No time for sit-down dinners or taking a day to goof off. She knew that feeling.

Which made her stop thinking about the man beside her so she could get back to the reason they'd come here in the first place. She'd only agreed to come with him since she hadn't wanted to go home without getting in a little productive work. Even if this was off the clock and even if her heart was leading more than her head.

The building in a border area of Bay Ridge looked like an old industrial type that had changed hands. Rows and rows of orange-colored doors lined up on long wide hallways with concrete floors. Emmett's unit was on the first floor above the parking garage and near an open catwalk that offered a feeble wisp of air now and then, thankfully.

"They close up at seven," he said as he shuffled pots

and pans and boxes. "We don't have much time. I should clean this thing out but…never can seem to make myself do it."

Belle helped him rearrange a few smaller boxes, noticing a pack of letters and some pictures. "Is it hard to let go of your parents' stuff?"

"Harder than I thought, yes. I kept what's here and what I have in my closet back at the apartment. Years of their lives and I have yet to accept fully that they're gone." He stopped and wiped at his brow. "They should have had more years together, but I guess I can fuss about that when I'm at the pearly gates."

Belle smiled at his gentle faith. Emmett presented himself as a big strong man but she could see that soft heart underneath.

"We'll all have questions then," she said on a soft note. "I'm glad I came to keep you company. I can't imagine my parents being gone."

No one should have to go through grief alone. She tried to imagine if something were to happen to her parents or siblings. How would she handle that? Hard to think about and yet, that day could come. Maybe he'd grown used to being a loner because the pain of being alone hurt so much. Tough to crack that facade.

When she heard a door opening down the way, out of habit, Belle checked the exits and entryways, then glanced out the one nearby window that had a good view of the street. Justice did the same, trained in much the same way as she'd been.

Dusk began to settle like dark velvet over the city while the last of the sunset left shadows that stretched across the eerie hulk of the nearby buildings. Outside, a hot wind whipped around corners, darting here and there in the simmering heat and blowing half-dead leaves off the trees. Traffic sounds echoed back into the open parking garage one floor below. Somewhere down the way, a car door slammed. Someone had a moving truck backed up to an open storage unit two rows over. Belle could hear the movers shouting at each other.

Emmett grunted and squinted at each container. Pushing away a table and two heavy chairs, he stretched toward the back of the square unit. "I think I see my dad's file box."

At least they didn't have to search long. Emmett's organization skills sure beat her own. Everything in this locker was neat and categorized so it didn't take long for him to find the bin marked *Emmett Marlin Gage*.

Popping the hinged lid up, he started methodically going through the batches of mustard-colored envelopes, each marked to show its contents.

Just outside the open unit door, Justice stood at attention since Belle had commanded him to guard. The big dog lifted his nose, sniffing the air with seasoned practice. He could pick up any number of scents around here, but she knew he'd zoom in on a human and alert them of any changes in what he sniffed.

She shouldn't be so jumpy, but her instincts repeated over and over that someone could be lurking around here. What if Emmett's cousin had gotten word that Emmett wanted to talk to him?

Why did she have that same feeling she'd had last night? That someone was watching her. It had to be Johnson, but something felt different.

"You're a junior?" she asked Emmett to keep her mind from going overboard on the speculations, noting the name on the bin he'd located way up top. "I'm surprised your dad's name hasn't popped up on our radar more."

"He went by E.M. Gage," Emmett explained while he pulled out and returned envelopes. "Never did like his name but my mom wanted to give it to me. He was Emmett Marlin Gage and I'm actually Emmett Michael Gage. We have the same initials but not the same name. A compromise—just one of the many lessons I learned from my parents."

"They sound like a wonderful couple," Belle said. "My parents are like that, always offering up life lessons even if none of us want to listen. I worry about my younger brother, Joaquin. He's going through a rebellious stage so he's disrespectful to my dad sometimes."

"How old is he?" Emmett asked as he moved bins and reorganized the tiny locker.

"Joaquin is fifteen, but he thinks he's older."

"Tough age but he'll learn."

"I'm afraid of what he'll learn," Belle said, her anxieties kicking in.

A pigeon fluttered down from the top of the squat building, startling Belle. Justice's ear perked up but he didn't move.

"Joaquin thinks he knows everything," she added.

"Ah, I remember that age."

Belle gave Emmett a twisted smile. "C'mon. You had to have been a Dudley Do-Right. I can't see you acting out like my brother's doing."

"So you consider me to be that boring?" he asked, grimacing. "I'll have you know I was indeed an upstanding citizen but I did have one of those summers a boy never forgets. But my dad never forgot, either. After those rebellious few months, he made sure I had a job lined up at the end of each school year."

Belle could imagine him as a teenager. Tall, with that sandy-blond hair and those piercing eyes. "I'm thinking you were a real charmer. Could have gotten into a lot of trouble and talked your way out of it."

"Actually, I have a hard time lying," he admitted. "I got in trouble, but I always fessed up. Took the rap to cover for a lot of friends who later turned out to be not-so-good friends. I wanted to be cool and wild, but my mom told me that God had a plan for me and it didn't include me trying to be something I wasn't. I guess I *am* a straight arrow. Boring but loyal." Then he grinned at her. "With the occasional rogue streak."

"Loyalty is a good trait," she replied, thinking her ex Percy Carolo hadn't had a loyal bone in his body but he had the rogue thing down in a bad way. Percy had wanted to be in law enforcement, but his hotheaded attitude didn't go over very well during training. "I'll take loyalty over being too wild and out of control any day."

"You seem loyal to your team," Emmett replied. "But you also seem very in control."

She moved another bin and then checked on her partner. Justice stood waiting patiently. "I love what I do. It's easy to be loyal when you want to do the best you can."

"A good trait." Then he gave her a determined glance. "But this kind of work takes its toll. Makes it hard to settle down."

"I hear that," she said, a deep disappointment coiling through her system. This man was heavily commitment shy.

Even though the place was climate-controlled, Belle noticed the sheen of sweat popping out on Emmett's upper lip and forehead. She also noticed that he was in good shape. Not an ounce of extra weight on him and mostly muscle. With a grunt, he lifted out one last filing envelope.

"Bingo." He held up a thick file envelope held together with strong bands. It was marked with the name *E.M. Gage* and the word *Private*.

Emmett shifted a few more boxes and containers. "I think it should all be in this one file I found. Might not be anything much in here, but Dad kept a few records and notes on cases he'd worked. If he knew anything of the McGregor murders, it might be in here. Okay, so are you ready to go somewhere and dig through this folder?"

Justice glanced back at them and then lifted his nose again. Belle heard a noise, like someone running on the industrial gray hallway floors.

Emmett put away the container and then tucked the file under his arm. Then he guided her out and secured the keypad on the door. In the next instant, Justice gave a soft woof of warning and then a shot rang out followed by a ding. A bullet pierced the top of the folded metal door.

Justice stood his ground and growled low while Emmett tugged Belle down into a crouch and automatically shielded her. "Are you okay?"

"Yes," she said, her weapon drawn, her eyes searching the long row of identical storage units but the hall light was muted, causing all of the shadows to merge and dance. "Do you think Lance Johnson followed us here?"

"Somebody did," Emmett replied on an angry growl of his own as he held her close to the floor. Pulling his shirt up, he shoved the file against his stomach and then tucked his shirt back in. "Let's get out of here."

Holding his weapon up as he scooted toward the other

side of the unit, he whispered, "I can't see anyone. We need to get to the truck."

"What about the few people in here?"

Emmett checked the keypad again. "Let's move along each row on this floor and try to find any bystanders. I know where a staircase to the left can take us down to the street level on the backside. Once we have people out and safe, we can circle back around."

"I can cover you," Belle said, eying both ends of the long aisle and the exit a few feet away. "You can make a run for it and warn people."

"I can do that," Emmett said, keeping his voice low. "But I'm not leaving you in here alone."

"Excuse me," Belle said. "I have Justice, and this is my job."

"I get that, but if we leave together, we have a better chance. What if the shooter isolates you in here? You'll be a sitting duck."

"Okay." Belle positioned herself on the other wall, by the door. "I'll get in place first, then motion to Justice. Justice can lead us out. He'll pick up any scents on the aisle or the stairwell. But we might have to split up to get help and we need to get everyone out of this building."

"Stay down and let's go." Emmett nodded and turned toward the first exit, a few yards away. A shot echoed over the building. Screams and people shouting soon followed.

Emmett went to his knees behind the container of files. "Those people are close by. That's not good."

"And we need to find this shooter fast," Belle said.

"Agreed."

Belle scanned the alley where they crouched in the narrow doorway of a closed closet. Another shot came close, hitting the ground at Emmett's feet. Justice waited in his position across from Belle, then barked and looked north. Belle heard people shouting and prayed they'd take cover until she and Emmett could help.

"I'm calling for backup," she whispered. "Then we move in."

Emmett nodded and watched while she made the call. "10-10. Shots fired inside City Wide Storage." She named the address and their location.

Justice barked again, his nose in the air. Then he glanced back at her, eager to go.

"Good boy," Belle said, shifting low to the ground. "I agree."

The shots were coming from inside the building and most likely this floor. Someone must have followed them and waited for an opportunity.

Emmett managed to dive into another corner across from them. "I can't see anyone."

Another shot rang out, pinging the concrete between units.

"I'm taking Justice along the open catwalk," Belle said. "You try to sneak out the back exit."

"Belle?"

"Emmett, let me do my job."

He nodded and scanned the corners. "I'll cover you until you're out of sight."

Lifting her head, she accepted that, then made another move. "Go," she ordered Justice. "Go. Find."

Justice started up the catwalk and then sniffed to the left, two aisles over. Giving him the silent signal to halt, Belle crouched down, then peeked around the row of storage closets and saw a movement on the other side of the long aisle. The shooter, inching closer.

A bullet whizzed past her head and Emmett returned

fire from behind her. Belle moved to the next corner, Justice following close, and waved Emmett to go. Then she sat back a few minutes and listened to running feet and shouts. She was about to make another run for it when she heard someone around the corner.

Justice emitted a low growl that told her he'd picked up the scent again. "Stay," she said, giving him a hand signal to back it up.

Belle lifted around the corner to peek.

A round of fire came at her and she retreated back, bullets pouncing and pinging past her and hitting the catwalk floor and concrete sides near the open air.

Then Emmett came up behind her, returning fire. "Belle, let's go!"

Belle lifted and took another glance. The man dropped down and rolled around the corner.

"I see the shooter, Emmett. I can circle around."

"No, I've alerted the manager and he's getting everyone out. They're all headed away and down the back stairs. That leaves us and him until backup gets here." Motioning to where the shots came from, he added, "We need to wait and let him come to us."

She didn't want to put anyone else in danger and if she went after the man now, he could grab a hostage to get him out of here. But she could go around and between units to get closer. But by the time she could sneak up on the shooter, they should have help surrounding the perimeters of the building.

"Let's try again," Emmett said when the sound of footsteps and voices settled down.

"Behind you," she said to Emmett. Then she shot once and did a quick sprint to the next set of units. She pointed to the last few rows of units across from them. "We can't get out unless we make a run to the very end units. And he'll be running that same way."

"Copy that." Emmett glanced up. "We need to make the stairs and get on a floor over him. Spot him from the catwalk."

Belle motioned okay. But footsteps took off up the way. "There he goes."

Belle saw a man dressed in dark colors moving in a crouch along the row where they'd planned to hide around the corner. "I think I can get in a shot." She got down and belly crawled as close to the corner as she could. "I'm going to send Justice in and then I'll make a move."

"Dangerous," Emmett said while sirens wailed in the distance. "Wait for backup."

"Justice can take him," she retorted. "I have to get over the fear of him being hurt again. He's trained, same as me."

Justice barked an agreement on that.

Belle lifted up and then shouted, "Attack."

The dog hurled through the air with teeth bared, but the man spun up and took off, his heavy footsteps echoing between units.

Justice followed in a fast, eager trot.

Belle hurried along with him, not sure where Emmett was since she'd taken off without him.

She made it around the corner and spotted the man going down the stairs to the parking garage. The opposite direction of where the manager had led the people away, thankfully.

Justice stayed on the man's trail with Belle sprinting behind him.

The man stopped at the bottom of the stairs when she and Justice reached the landing. "Stop," Belle called out.

"Put the gun down." He fired but missed. Then he took off running.

Emmett came up behind her and fired after him. They spotted the man as he reached the other end of the parking lot where a sign stated Employee Parking Only. He hurled over barriers and sprinted toward a navy-colored car, Justice racing after him.

Justice kept barking and snarling. The man turned, his features shadowed by dusk, and shot haphazardly into the air. Then he opened the battered car door and jumped into the vehicle. A moment later Justice jumped up against the driver's side door, all teeth and bark.

The economy car had seen better days, but it cranked and revved before heading out of a small exit on the east side of the building.

Belle shouted to Justice to halt and ran with all her might, praying Justice wouldn't get shot or hit. But the car peeled out and skidded around a corner before she could get in a shot.

"Come," she called to Justice. Justice snarled but he retreated back toward her. Belle heard the car's squealing tires as it sped away.

"Did you get the license number?" Belle asked Emmett as he came hurrying behind her.

"No, I couldn't make it out in the dark," he said, stopping to catch his breath. "We should have chased him in the truck."

"We wouldn't have made it, anyway," she said, gulping in air. "Justice almost had him."

Belle sent a description out over the radio. Officers came running and surrounded them. Belle and Emmett quickly gave an update. Reports of officers in pursuit came back.

After they'd secured the building and made sure everyone else was safe, Belle turned to Emmett. "At least I got a good look at that messed up door on the driver's side."

"Did he look like your man?"

"I can't say," she admitted. "He had on gray baggy pants and a lightweight hoodie and big sunglasses. Could have been anyone."

"But only a few would shoot at us. Namely, two that I can think of."

"You mean the two men we're after?" Belle asked as they turned toward Emmett's truck.

"Yep." Emmett made sure she and Justice were both inside before he got in and put the vehicle in drive. "Lance Johnson and Randall Gage."

"But Randall doesn't know we're looking for him," Belle said, wondering again if Emmett had been in touch with Randall.

"If he's in the area and he's seen us together, it wouldn't be hard for him to figure out. He might have been warned by someone in cahoots with him. I've put out the word so people might have been asking around."

"Would your cousin shoot at us just to scare us? Or would he shoot to kill? Because we know Lance Johnson is a lousy shot and so was this person today."

"Who knows at this point," Emmett said. "They both might have motive to keep us quiet. But you're right. That person had every opportunity to shoot to kill and he missed."

Belle let that realization soak in as they headed out of the storage lot. She could see Lance Johnson wanting to kill her but Emmett's cousin? And would he really shoot his own relative?

If he killed once, he could easily kill again.

Then word came over the radio that they'd lost the car in pursuit. Apparently, whoever this was knew his way around Brooklyn enough to elude a police chase. Where had he gone?

"I'm liking Lance Johnson for this," she told Emmett. "Let's find Randall and bring him in before we jump to any more conclusions," she suggested. "It's a stretch that this could be him, but he did live here once and could be tailing us, too."

"Yeah, same as it was a stretch that you'd find one of my relatives who might be involved in a cold case from twenty years ago?"

Emmett had a point. What were the odds?

She needed to keep this case and all the facts front and center and get the job done. They had to find both Lance Johnson and Randall Gage soon. Because not only was she in physical danger on all sides, but her heart was becoming more and more open to getting to know Emmett better, too.

She sure didn't need to add dealing with an interesting, hard-to-read man to her to-do list.

SEVEN

By the time they went their separate ways, Belle was too tired to focus on anything but sleep. Her boss had called her and reprimanded her heavily about not listening to orders. "I'm not telling you again, Belle. Stay home tomorrow or I'll put you filing away evidence down in the basement."

"Yes, sir," she'd replied while they stood inside Gavin's office. "I didn't think this would turn into an ordeal."

"Someone is trying to kill you, Belle. *That* is an ordeal and one you need to take seriously. You went out with the marshal when you were supposed to be off duty and recuperating."

She didn't argue that she also wanted to take Randall Gage seriously. But she did want to stay on the case and since she didn't want to lose this job, she had to settle down and wait for at least twenty-four hours or risk being in even worse trouble.

"I'll look these files over tonight," Emmett told her back at the precinct, once Sarge was done with her. "If I find anything helpful, I'll call you tomorrow."

"Did he let you have it, too?" she asked Emmett.

"Not in the same way. He mostly glared at me and then asked about the shooter. But he did say he's got people searching for the car we described. It seems to have disappeared off the face of the earth."

"I should be out there, too."

"No. You're supposed to go home. Don't push it, Belle."

Emmett hadn't exactly ordered her around. The concern in his voice held her steady. That and the exhaustion taking over her whole system.

"Okay," she said in sharp acceptance. "I'm leaving right now. Justice and I will watch an old movie."

"Now I know you're tired. You didn't argue with me."

She smiled and then made a face at him. But he was right.

Her throat muscles were still sore, tight and burning and her whole body seemed locked in a death grip she couldn't shake. She'd held it all in but now it shouted at her with every step she took. Plus, she needed to see her family. She'd been making excuses since the other night when Emmett had come to her apartment with her. Had that only been last night?

Usually, she'd poke her head in at breakfast, grab a piece of toast or a bagel and head out to work. Then she'd stop by at night and nibble on leftovers and give her parents a kiss before crashing in her own place. Her mother started speculating if she didn't show.

Sure that Cara had reported the whole scene of her and Emmett in the dark kitchen of their parents' home, Belle needed to make an appearance before she could go to her own apartment and get some sleep. Her mom would come looking and then Belle would get a lecture about settling down and getting married. Her mother prayed she'd give up her dangerous job and find something more suitable. That would never work. Belle wasn't cut out to be an office worker or a stay-at-home mother. She needed to be out in the city, helping other people.

Around nine o'clock, she entered her parents' apartment, using the key she always had on hand, Justice following excitedly since he loved her family.

"Belle, is that you?"

"It's me, Mamá."

Gina Montera lapsed into Spanish, fussing over her oldest daughter and telling her to sit. She needed to eat.

"I'm not hungry," Belle replied, slipping down onto a dining chair, the feeling of being home and safe overtaking her. "I just wanted to report in. Things have been kind of wild at work this week."

"I'm your mother, not your boss," Gina pointed out, her short dark curls framing her oval face. "You don't check in with me, you come by to see your poor mother, show me you are alive and okay. This is my one rule." Pulling out sliced turkey and sandwich bread, she shoved a plate in front of Belle and then stared at her neck, her dark gaze slamming against Belle's face. "What happened to you? And don't tell me you have some stalker but I'm not to worry about it. Mothers worry."

Belle cringed and chewed on a chunk of spicy turkey. "I got into a fight with a bad guy and I don't think he's done with me."

Gina shook her head and put a hand to her mouth. "He did this to you? Is he the one who left that envelope? The one you warned us about?"

"I think so, but I'm fine," Belle said, lifting her collar a bit. "And I have people watching over all of you, too." He grabbed me at the park, but I had help."

"The man your sister saw you with last night?"

"Sí." Belle nibbled the bread, then took a drink of tea.

"He's a US marshal who's helping me with a cold case. We had a meeting and he came along just in time."

"I'm thankful for that." Gina flicked Belle's uniform collar. "As if you could hide that from your mother. You need to settle down and get married. This is not the work for you."

"We've discussed this," Belle said for the hundredth time. "I like what I do. I like protecting people."

"But not yourself." Pointing to Justice, she asked, "Where was this one when you were attacked?"

Justice's ears went up and his dark eyes widened as if he wanted to explain but felt too fuzzy to do so. He let out a soft whimper and then put his head back on his paws.

Belle didn't want to go into detail about Justice getting hit with a tranquilizer dart because she'd get another round of fear and condemnation. "Nearby, but Justice did his best and between him and my friend, I'm here and I'm okay. Sorry I missed dinner again."

She stood and stretched. "Is Papá in bed already?"

Gina nodded. "He's tired. Your brother and he had words again."

"About?"

"Joaquin seems to think he can run around with whomever he pleases. The crowd he's with now is not a good one."

"I'll talk to him again," Belle said on a frustrated note. "He could get into serious trouble if he keeps this up. I won't always be able to run interference." She thought about Randall Gage and felt sure Emmett's father and Emmett, too, had done their best to help him when they could. But the man was in his sixties now and could be getting away with murder.

How did a person live with that kind of guilt?

"We both try to tell him this," her mother replied, tears in her eyes. "But your brother thinks he knows more than we do. He is stubborn and determined."

"Well, so am I," Belle replied before she kissed her mom on the head. "Anita and Cara?"

"Up in their room, supposedly going to bed early since they start summer jobs this week working at Uncle Rico's café."

Belle nodded at that. She remembered earning money working at Rico's Café just around the corner from their apartment building. Her uncle had encouraged her to follow her dreams and never forget her roots.

"I'm glad they're working and close by at that." Then she pushed her plate away and took a long sip of her mother's tart lemonade. "Has anyone come around this week? Asking questions? Anything like that?"

"No, but we're watching carefully, just as you said."

"I'm so sorry, Mamá. I don't want it spilling over on all of you."

"You'd tell me if there's more right?"

"I'll tell you if you need to know, yes, Mamá."

Gina shook her head. "Now I'll worry."

"Don't. You know I watch out for all of you."

"What about you?" Gina asked. "Does your new friend watch out for you?"

"He tries," Belle admitted, thinking about how she and Emmett had somehow meshed in spite of being forced together in a strange way. "If I let him."

"You need to start letting more," Gina reminded her. "I want grandchildren before I'm too old."

Belle accepted a motherly kiss and then went down to her place with her mother's parting words in her head. Did she want children?

Emmett came to mind again and she shoved that image away. She would not put a man like Emmett Gage in the same thought with a passel of kids. She'd only met him a little over twenty-four hours ago. Not much time to plan out a future.

And way too soon after she'd dumped Percy Carolo, a man who wanted to be a police officer but didn't want to accept the rank-and-file authority that required. She wouldn't compete to prove her worth with another law enforcement man, even if this one actually knew what he was doing and seemed to treat her equally.

Nope, she wouldn't go there. Not tonight. Too tired, sore and sleepy. But her mind whirled with why Lance Johnson had it in for her. Then she moved to the puzzle of Emmett's cousin Randall and why he might murder a married couple and leave the young child, Penny, who'd been home at the time, unharmed. Could he have done the same thing again two months ago with the Emerys and little Lucy?

The two couples had little in common and didn't know one another. She knew based on her video phone call with the Emerys' landlords, the O'Malleys, that the couple had been rowdy renters who were behind on their bills. Lucy, appearing unkempt, had often been seen playing alone in the yard. Bradley and Penny McGregor hadn't had a stable childhood, either. Both sets of parents were neglectful. But that didn't constitute murder unless the killer thought the parents deserved what they got and had a soft spot for children. Seemed far-fetched, but all ideas for motives were welcome.

That made her think of Emmett again. He'd be good with children. He had a strong work ethic and a solid faith.

Your parents would be so proud of you, Emmett.

Why did she feel that Emmett had something to prove and that something meant he didn't want to settle down?

Maybe tomorrow or weeks from now, she'd let that image of Emmett's silvery eyes and nice smile slip back into her psyche. But for now, they had a lot of work to do and none of it involved him being in her future.

Her phone buzzed at seven the next morning.

"Hello?" Belle said, still sleepy.

"It's Emmett. I got called out on a case. An escapee we've been trying to locate for six months. We've got a strong tip that he's hiding out in Long Island. Not sure when I'll be done here."

"Go," she said, "And be safe."

"How are you?"

"I was good until someone woke me up."

"Sorry, just wanted to check. I'll call later."

"Okay. Meantime, I'll do some online research and try to behave." Then she said, "Hey, Emmett, would Randall go out of his way to protect a child?"

A pause and then, "Maybe. He had a tough life with a tough dad. Are you onto something?"

"I don't know. Just wondering why the murderer left Penny there with a stuffed animal. I could ask the same about Lucy Emery, but since we only have DNA evidence from the McGregor murders, I'm focusing on the cold case."

"Good question." Then he let out a breath. "You know, Randall did some work as a carnie. He worked one of the games where the prizes were stuffed animals."

Belle jotted that in her notes, remembering Emmett's earlier reminder that Randall liked to collect toys and trinkets. "So he loved stuffed animals and also had access to them. Interesting. I'm going to pretend to be resting while I try to piece things together."

"Right. You're something else, Montera."

Belle hung up, wondering what that *something else* might be. A good something or a pain-in-the-neck something? He'd given her enough warnings to show her he was unavailable. Or at least, emotionally unavailable.

She actually smiled. Maybe she should date more just to prepare her for when the really good ones came along. She had a feeling Emmett was a good one but that was beside the point.

She stretched and got up, then turned on the coffee pot. Throwing on a robe over her nightgown, she let Justice out into the dog-run and gave him some playtime in the small square yard with the tall white fence. Belle had a nice Adirondack chair with soft cushions to sit in when she wasn't chasing Justice around. Now she sat there with her coffee and took in the scent of her mother's roses and the neighbor's breakfast.

"Belle?"

She glanced up to see her twin sisters smiling down from the fire escape, their long dark hair falling in silky waves around their faces. "Hey."

"Mamá says come eat breakfast. She made blueberry pancakes and your favorite scrambled eggs."

"I'll be up soon," Belle said with a grin.

"Where did you meet that hunk that Cara caught you with?" Anita asked with a smug smile.

"At work."

"Are you two a thing?"

"No, we are not a thing. He's on a case with my unit."

Cara grinned. "So? You've been on a date?"

"No date. I just met him like two days ago and we were after a very nasty person. That doesn't qualify as a date."

Her sister shrugged. "It could, if you flirt a little."

"Hey, I don't flirt at work."

"Maybe you should," Cara suggested.

They both whirled when their father called out in his gruff voice, "Time to eat."

Belle got Justice in and they both trudged upstairs to enjoy an early breakfast with the whole family. Except Joaquin.

Apparently, he was sleeping late now that school was out.

Since Belle had the day off, she intended to have a strongly worded talk with her brother.

EIGHT

Belle was back at work in the training yard the next day, taking Justice through the paces. Her partner seemed as anxious as she was to get rolling again, despite the unsettling talk she'd had with her brother last night. Joaquin didn't want to listen to her warnings about finding a summer job and staying away from the group of kids who roamed the streets looking for trouble night and day.

She'd have to keep on him whether he liked it or not. Right now, she wanted to finish this workout and get back to her desk to try to find more information on the two thorns in her side—Randall Gage and Lance Johnson.

Justice must have felt her anxiety. The German shepherd was all in on running through the obstacle course out in the training yard. It was hard to keep a good working dog down.

"That a boy," she called as the eager K-9 showed his worth by walking across ladders and flying over low walls before searching through barrels and containers for hidden evidence. Then they practiced circle-and-bark and worked on reasonable force. The circle-and-bark was just that—he'd keep circling the cornered suspect and bark until he had further instructions. The reasonable force meant Justice wouldn't bite until ordered to do so as a last resort. A well-trained K-9 meant less unnecessary injuries and fewer lawsuits for the department. And that meant she had to be on high alert all the time, too. Justice trusted her to make the right calls.

Wishing they could have cornered the perp in the storage warehouse yesterday, Belle gave Justice due credit for trying to capture the man, at least. Justice would have taken the shooter if she'd shouted the attack order in time. But the man had sprinted to the car and that was that.

She made up for her mistake this morning by pushing both Justice and herself to the limit.

"We've still got it," Belle told her excited partner once they'd gone through the paces. "Playtime now."

Justice knew what that meant. After a short game of tug-of-war to show him that he would always be rewarded after hard work, they freshened up and Belle hurried to her cubicle. "Time to find the truth."

Emmett was waiting for her, dressed as usual in his dark polo shirt and khakis, his badge hanging from a lanyard around his neck, his dark baseball hat on the desk in front of him.

"Morning," he said, standing when she reached her chair. "I brought fresh coffee."

"You're going to give me a bad rep," she said, gratitude in her tone. "My team members will be jealous and call me a diva."

"You, a diva? I doubt that." He opened his own coffee and took a sip. "I saw you two out on the practice field. Pretty impressive."

Justice lifted his head and shot them a doggy smile.

"Yes, you, too," Emmett said, grinning at the big dog.

Belle wanted to smile, too. So he'd been watching them? That made little tingles of awareness move down her spine. It had been a while since a handsome man had shown her any interest, even if it was only the professional kind.

"We have to do a certain amount of training each week to stay on track and stay certified," she explained. "Can't slack off or get too complacent."

"No, because the bad guys never do."

"Well, I'm thinking the one who's after me has some issues there. He's kind of trigger-happy but also haphazard. He'll mess up soon enough."

"Just remember he has serious upper body strength," Emmett replied, touching a hand to his collar. "I didn't enjoy seeing his hands on your throat."

"Good point. I'm going to check the gyms around his apartment. The man obviously works out. Probably did in prison, too. I don't remember him being so beefy the first time Justice and I took him down."

"I guess he remembers you, though."

"Too well. I guess prison didn't suit him so now he blames me. Too bad he's going back there."

Belle finished her daily workout report and then gave her full attention to Emmett. "So first, did you find the escapee?"

"Yes. He's back in a warm, cozy cell with a nice downtown view of nothing but bars. He won't be roaming around on the sly anymore."

"Good, and second, did you find anything in your dad's files?"

Emmett sighed and leaned back in the chair across from hers. "Yes. In fact, I'm waiting to talk to see—"

"Marshal Gage, Belle, a word," Gavin called from his office.

"Him," Emmett finished, getting up and waiting for her to do the same.

"Coming, sir," Belle called after giving Justice the sign to follow.

Gavin stood waiting for them and then shut the door. "Deputy Marshal, what did you find last night?"

Sarge was obviously still sore at them for going rogue the other day. Belle wanted to hear what Emmett had to say so she refrained from apologizing again.

"I went over the few bits of information I could find," Emmett explained. "My father never brought home official files, of course. He always logged in any evidence or notes and put them in the evidence room just like any good officer would."

"But?" Belle asked, wondering.

"But he kept a personal notebook to back up what he saw each time he made an arrest or got involved in a case."

"Just as a reference?" Gavin asked, his scowl not so sharp now.

"Yes," Emmett replied. "And because, unfortunately, he worked with some pretty shifty cops at one time."

"Do any of those shifty cops have a place in our investigation?" Gavin asked.

"No, but I'm trying to establish that he had his reasons for keeping thorough notes and that served him well for many years."

Gavin nodded. "Your dad sounds like a good cop. What did you find?"

Belle gave her superior a slanted glance, but Gavin remained as stoic as a rock. He wanted answers.

Emmett sat up and pulled out a black notebook. "I have a few notations. *April 20, 2000. I got a call from*

Randall today. Haven't heard a word from him in five years. But he didn't have much to say when push came to shove. Seemed nervous and rambled a lot. Just said that he was heading out."

"Heading out?" Gavin took the notebook and studied the handwriting. "This would have been around the time of the McGregor murders."

Emmett nodded. "Could have been Randall's way of telling my dad he was leaving the state of New York. I did some digging and found out that's the first time he went to Pennsylvania. Worked around the farms there, even worked with the Amish a few years. But he drifted away and lost contact, as I've already reported."

"What else do you have?" Gavin asked, handing the notebook back to Emmett.

"Another reference right before my father retired. *Randall's in trouble again, but I can't help him. He won't tell me what he's done but he's in a bad way about something that happened long ago. Couldn't get him to meet with me.*"

"That was in the fall of 2015," Emmett continued. "My dad passed away a couple of months after that."

"That's not much to go on," Belle said. "It shows your dad tried to keep in touch with Randall but if Randall told him anything regarding the cold-case murders, it went to his grave with him."

Gavin nodded. "Why would your father leave such cryptic notes? Maybe he was noting times and dates while he protected Randall, maybe even knew he was on the run and where he was headed."

Emmett shook his head and stood up. "You didn't know my dad. He was straitlaced and hard-nosed. He went by the book, always. Never had a speck of scandal in his thirty years of being in law enforcement. You can easily verify that."

Gavin stood, too. "We have to consider every angle. Trust me, I've been through this and it's not easy." Shrugging, he said, "Even the best of us try to do the right things for the wrong reasons. If your dad had a soft spot for Randall, he might have overlooked or purposely left out some important details."

Emmett shook his head. "I'm telling you—it's not like that. You both said you didn't find any connection in the official files that could show my dad was aware of these murders. This murder case might have been common knowledge, but my dad was never part of the investigation. So stop going down that rabbit hole."

Gavin shot Belle a reluctant glance. "Duly noted but we all need to stay on this and go back over every detail. Maybe your father destroyed a few journal entries."

Emmett scrubbed a hand down his chin, his expression sharpening with anger. "I'll keep reading my dad's notes but I'm telling you both, he wouldn't have covered up a double homicide even if his own mother had done it."

Belle reached out to him. "Emmett, I'm sorry."

"Sorry?" His eyes narrowed. "You people tracked me down and questioned me, made me feel like a suspect even though I had nothing to do with this and now you're starting in on my father? We can't help that Randall is related to us and none of us—not my dad nor me or my mom—has any inkling that Randall could have been involved in something so horrible. I understand you need my cooperation and you need me to find Randall so I can get fresh DNA to verify what you've found. I'm on that. But you need to lay off my dad. Keep him out of this."

Pointing his finger at the notebook in his other hand,

he said, "If my dad had heard word of him being a suspect, he would have noted it here and he would have at least kept the news clippings, or anything to tie to Randall. Then he would have worked to bring him in. But the news reports and the official reports all indicate *suspect unknown*."

He gave Belle a frustrated stare and then whirled toward the door. "I have my own cases to get back to but I'd appreciate it if you'd keep me informed if you find Randall. And I'm duty bound to do the same—I won't cover for him or help him escape. He needs to pay if he did this, but he is innocent until proven guilty. Understand?"

Belle glanced from his departing back to Gavin's shocked face. "Sir?"

"Let him go for now. He's right, of course. We just need to find something on Randall Gage. Anything that can either clear the man or condemn him. We're stalling out here."

"I'll get back on it," she said, motioning to Justice. "But we just lost a strong contact. I don't know if Emmett *will* come around anymore."

"We've established enough to do this on our own, Belle."

"Have we?" she questioned.

"Are you disputing me?"

"No, sir." She shrugged. "He was kind of growing on me, though. He was a good resource."

Gavin gave her one of his measured stares, but Belle met his gaze with one of her own. "The man saved my life. We kind of bonded."

"Well, that's good," Gavin replied on a dry note. "Once you've solved this case, you can be friends with the deputy. How 'bout that?"

"That might work, sir," she said. Then she hurried out the door, hoping to find Emmett.

But Emmett Gage was long gone from the Brooklyn K-9 Unit headquarters.

Would she ever see him again?

Gavin didn't give her much time to think about Emmett. He ordered her and Noelle Orton, a rookie who used to be a K-9 trainer, to search once again for Lance Johnson. Noelle had been taking less public assignments since her K-9 partner, Liberty, had broken up two major gun-smuggling operations at the airport. Because of that, a gunrunner had put a bounty of ten-thousand dollars on Liberty's head. So neither of them had had much street time lately.

"A car matching the description of the one you and Emmett saw last night at the storage warehouse was located near a building in Canarsie about thirty minutes ago. It's not far from Johnson's last known address. He might be around. Take Noelle and Liberty with you. Noelle can use the experience and Liberty needs to stay sharp, too. Since this is a low-profile case, they both should be safe."

Now Belle and Noelle along with their partners were walking the perimeters of the older neighborhood. Noelle was tall and strong, her long dark hair in its usual low bun below her cap. Her yellow Lab, Liberty, had a telltale black splotch on her ear, which made the targeted K-9 all too easy to identify. They'd have to be vigilant for Liberty's sake. As they walked, Belle spotted the car immediately and took a picture. Justice sniffed the vehicle and turned to give her a doleful affirmative.

"Dark navy economy car. Damage to the driver-side

door and a deep white gash along that side of the vehicle. That's the car the shooter used to get away yesterday," she told Noelle. "Has to be the same one."

After radioing confirmation and the car's license plate number, she turned to Noelle. "We can't search it without a warrant, and I didn't get the license number yesterday. So we'll have to wait to find out who owns the vehicle. But we can check Johnson's apartment building again."

Noelle's green eyes widened. "Let's go."

Liberty appeared to be just as eager to get some action.

The valiant Lab didn't know she was in any danger from gunrunners who wanted to stop her from being so good at her job. She was always ready and willing to take down criminals. Justice trotted along beside Liberty, obviously smitten.

"I hear that," Belle said to Noelle's gung ho attitude. "I want this guy off the streets."

They walked back to the big old square brick apartment building. "The super is not friendly," she warned Noelle. She'd already told her colleague about the super wearing a ring that looked like the one her attacker had been wearing. "We'll see if he has on jewelry today."

But they never made it up onto the stoop. Gunfire raged all around them, sending Belle and Noelle running up the cracked concrete steps to hide behind the stone railings.

"Stay down," Belle told Noelle. "I'm going to see if I can get a visual on the shooter."

She ran to the other side of the porch, thinking being shot at was getting tiresome. But after scanning the area, she couldn't see anyone hiding on a roof or lurking around a corner.

The whole neighborhood went quiet as people slammed

their doors and turned down their music and televisions. Belle waited a couple of beats and then moved to the other end of the porch.

When she heard footsteps in the alley behind the narrow building, she signaled for Justice. He came charging and waited for her next command.

Then she motioned to Noelle and pointed toward the other side of the property. "Around back."

Noelle and Liberty headed in one direction and Belle took Justice over the railing on her side of the house.

When she rounded the corner, she saw a figure dressed in dark clothes running away. "Go," she ordered Justice. They both took off running to the right.

Belle called out. "NYPD. Stop!"

But once again, the shooter eluded them. Justice ran to a high wooden fence and barked. Belle caught up but found the fence chain-locked from the other side.

Noelle and Liberty came running. "What happened?"

"I think they went over this fence. Or had some help getting inside," Belle replied, irritation coloring her words. "I'm not enjoying being shot at every time I turn around."

Noelle's eyebrows lifted as she glanced around the hot, dank alley. "What if that shot wasn't for you, Belle?"

Noelle pointed to Liberty. "You're not the only K-9 officer in danger these days."

"You think they came here for Liberty?" Belle asked, a chill going down her back.

"I don't know," Noelle replied. "But the first shot hit pretty close to where Liberty was standing." Shrugging, she said, "We were both in plain sight and the shot hit near my partner. I try to take her out only on support cases, like this one, but maybe someone is following me—someone who wants the bounty on Liberty's head."

"Thankfully the shooter missed," Belle replied. "Let's get a team out here to scavenge for bullet fragments and any prints we can find."

"Like that'll be a piece of cake," Noelle replied. But she made the call.

Shaking her head, Belle wondered when they'd gone from protecting the public to trying to keep each other alive.

NINE

"So the vehicle does belong to Lance Johnson," Belle told Noelle later that day after they'd gone back to the precinct. "But of course, he's nowhere to be found. Nor was the building super today, either."

They'd gone inside after the shooting and found the office door locked and the reception area empty. None of the residents wanted to talk much about anything.

"Maybe they're in cahoots," Noelle said, letting out a tired breath. "Or maybe today's shooting had nothing to do with your suspect."

"I'm glad Liberty is okay," Belle told her friend when they walked up to the vending machine to get a snack since they'd missed lunch. "Hard to believe someone could be so evil as to try to kill a dog."

"Not just any dog," Noelle replied. "But a trained officer of the law. If Liberty's gone, these gun smugglers win. They tend to forget, however, we train dogs to work with us all the time. I'm going to protect Liberty with all I've got but if they harm her, I'll work with another K-9 in Liberty's honor to find them once and for all."

Belle lifted her chin in acknowledgment. "You're a good officer, Noelle. Liberty is blessed to have you."

"I feel the same about her," Noelle said. "But speaking

of that, what happened to that hunky shadow that's been following you around for the last few days. You haven't mentioned Emmett at all today."

Belle tugged the potato chip bag out of the ornery machine and lowered her head. "Nope. We're still hoping he can help us track down the one cousin who lived in Bay Ridge at the time of the McGregor murders. But the deputy marshal is not happy with us since he thinks we may taint his father's memory. He was a police officer."

"Will you?"

"I hope not. It's been hard on Emmett. I think he regrets not keeping up with his cousin."

"Family is complicated," Noelle replied. "But you and the marshal seem chummy."

"We're friends," Belle said. "And we have to get this case figured out. Not to mention, the man's saved my life twice now."

"Sounds like a good person to have in your corner."

"Emmett is a good person," Belle said, something in her heart hurting too much. "He's doing his job right now, nothing more."

Noelle shot her a glance. "Have you two grown close?"

"Yes, I guess almost being choked to death brings out my friendly side."

Noelle shook her head. "I'm glad Emmett came along when he did."

"So am I," Belle admitted. "For more reasons than one."

Belle took Justice home and fed him. Then she took him out back for a while. Justice ran off to explore while she sat down in her bright blue chair and enjoyed the last of the warm sun on her skin.

"Hi," her sister Anita said, trotting down the outside stairs to the yard to join Belle.

"Hi, yourself," Belle said. "How ya doing?"

Anita, the quieter of the twins, sank down in the grass and twirled a strand of her long dark hair. "I guess I'm okay. I like working for Uncle Rico's café, but Cara flirts with all the busboys. It's embarrassing."

"Your sister is a bit more outgoing than you."

"You think?"

Belle laughed at that. "I know she's a pain at times, but you two are to always stick together coming and going to work since Uncle Rico put you on the same schedule."

"We are for now," Anita said. "But I want extra hours and Cara wants the least amount of hours. So…"

"Have you noticed anyone strange hanging around?" Belle asked, fear for her sisters on her mind. "I need to hear daily reports."

Anita shrugged and tugged at a tear in her jeans. "I don't know. I mean, maybe. We've been working there all week but today, this creepy guy kept sneering at us. He even asked why there were two of us."

Belle's antenna went up but she stayed calm. "What did he look like?"

Anita made a twisted face. "Big. You know, the kind who hangs out in the gym a lot? Thick hair but he wore weird glasses."

"Sunshades?"

Anita nodded and adjusted her baggy tank top. "The kind that go from light to dark. Kind of freaked me out."

Could her attacker have been wearing glasses with transitional lenses?

That would explain the sunshades the other day, Belle

thought. The late afternoon sun had been bright right before that rain had hit in the park.

"So he didn't take the glasses off when he came inside?"

"No. They were dark and then they got light enough for me to see his eyes before he shoved a hat on his head. Do you think he's the one who's after you, Belle?"

Belle always walked a fine line between keeping her family safe and keeping them unaware of most of what she dealt with on a daily basis. So she had to tread lightly here. She'd sent someone to watch the café but she'd heard nothing. If Gavin would let her, she'd stake out the place herself. But she didn't want her sisters in further danger.

"He sounds like him," she explained to Anita. "He's got it in for me so he could try to harass any of you, too. He's kind of bulky, like you mentioned, and he wears dark sunshades. Never takes them off." Calling to Justice, she worked hard to keep her voice normal. "Do you remember the color of his eyes?"

Anita twisted her chin. "Hazel, maybe?"

Grabbing her phone, she showed her sister the mug shot she'd been using to ID Johnson. "Is this the man?"

Anita took the phone. "That could be him, *sí*."

Lance Johnson's rap sheet described him as having dark shaggy hair and hazel eyes. But when he'd attacked her in the park, Belle remembered his hair as being shorter. She needed a positive ID.

"Do you think he'll try something?" Anita asked, apprehension coloring her question.

"I don't know. But we have to check every lead. You just let me take care of this. I'll speak to Uncle Rico, too. You both might need to stay away from work for a few days, or at least continue to be driven back and forth."

"Okay," Anita said. "Uncle Rico watches out for us, anyway. He's afraid the waiters will hit on us, you know?"

"I do know," Belle said. "I worked there a few summers. You find him if this man returns or call me on my cell, okay?"

Anita nodded. "I will, I promise."

Stretching to hide the fear clawing her insides, Belle added, "Just be aware and stick together. I have a patrol car watching this street. Don't go anywhere on foot until this is over. I need to tell Joaquin that, too, and make him understand."

"That sounds serious," Anita relied.

"Comes with the territory." Then she knocked on her sister's arm with a gentle fist. "Remember what I've always told you and Cara. Be aware and use all the self-defense tricks I've taught you. Understand?"

"Sí, bonita."

Belle's cell buzzed while she smiled at the endearment. "I need to answer this," she told Anita as she stood. "And Justice should get inside and get settled. Wanna come in?"

"No, thanks." Her sister hopped up. "I'm reading a really good book. After dinner, I'm going to finish it."

Belle nodded as Anita took off up the stairs. Then she scanned the small yard and street behind their building but didn't see anything out of the ordinary. "Justice, come," she called before hitting Accept. "Belle Montera."

"Hi. It's Emmett."

His grainy voice shouldn't have made her pulse get so jumpy, but the man seemed to have a strange effect on her.

"Hi," she replied after shutting the door and locking it. Trying to sound unconcerned and nonchalant, she asked, "What's up?"

He let out a breath. "I wanted to apologize for storming out on you and Sergeant Sutherland this morning. This whole business has ruffled my feathers and made me see that I don't have much family left. It's hard to accept Randall might be a killer."

Belle's heart stopped jumping but the jitters were replaced with a steady throbbing beat. She felt sorry for Emmett. He didn't have anyone close in his life from what he'd told her.

"Hey, you want to come over so we can talk?" she asked against her better judgment and being bolder than she'd ever been with any other man. "I didn't like how we left things this morning, either."

"Are you sure?"

"Of course I'm sure, Emmett. We've been through a lot together this week. How about tonight we just hang out like friends do?"

"Friends? Are we still even that?"

"Hey, once you've been chased and shot at together a few times, I think there's a rule about it making you friends for life."

His chuckle kicked down her backbone. "I didn't know about that rule."

"Well, it triples when you save my life not once, but twice."

"I didn't save you, Belle. You're good at saving yourself."

"Then it's my turn to save you from being bored and lonely and concerned about all of this. Come on over and we'll relax. Maybe watch a corny movie."

"I haven't watched a movie in years."

"How about *The Fugitive*?"

"You're funny, you know that. I'll be there soon. Want me to bring dinner?"

Belle thought about her empty refrigerator. "Yes. Surprise me."

"I can do that."

She ended the call and hurried to call Gavin regarding what her sister had told her. By the time Emmett arrived, she was clean and wearing a blue T-shirt, old well-worn jeans and slip-on sandals.

He'd just walked in with two bags of Chinese takeout when Belle saw her mother coming down the stairs. She couldn't shut the door in her mom's face.

"Belle, come up for dinner," Gina said, stopping when she saw Emmett standing there.

Belle cringed as her petite mother's eyes moved over Emmett until she had to lean her head back to actually see his face. "Oh, you have company?" Then she added in Spanish, "*Él es muy guapo.*"

Belle cringed again, knowing that Emmett spoke Spanish. But her mom was right. The man was very handsome. She rolled her eyes.

He grinned and said, "Is this your beautiful mother, Belle?"

Gina's dimples went into overdrive. "*Sí*, I am her mother and whatever you have in that bag, bring it upstairs and we'll share our food if you'll share yours."

"Mom, I don't think that's a good idea," Belle said, motioning Emmett inside.

"No, I think that's a great idea," Emmett said, clearly enjoying this. "I bought enough fried rice and dumplings to feed a large crowd."

"We have a large crowd," Belle said on a defeated note. "Which you will soon find out."

She shouldn't subject the man to her family all at once. But Emmett needed people and her family was friendly and loving if nothing else. She'd set them all clear on why Emmett was here later. Friends. They were just friends.

"I can't wait," he replied. "Mrs. Montera, may I escort you up to dinner."

Her mother actually giggled. "You certainly may. And a gentleman, too," she said over her shoulder to Belle.

"Don't worry. I know the way," Belle said, motioning for Justice to follow them.

She wanted to update Emmett on what her sister had told her but that would have to wait. She'd called Gavin almost immediately and he had an extra patrol car canvasing the area around her uncle's café and keeping tabs on Johnson's apartment. Lance Johnson was good at hiding and sneaking in and out of places, but he'd slip up one day.

And Belle would be there waiting for him when he did.

Right now, she had no choice but to follow Emmett upstairs.

She was hungry, and he had their food.

This could get interesting, but the smile on his face was so worth the trouble her family would put them both through. She only hoped that once they had criminal matters under control, they could still hang out together. He needed people, and she needed a good friend. Nothing more.

But what if there could be more? Did she want that?

TEN

Emmett listened to the conversation flowing around him in both English and Spanish, glad he had a general understanding of what was being said. It had been a while since he'd been surrounded by a big, loud family.

Belle kept glancing across the table at him, checking to see how he was holding up. So far, her family had gone on with their meal as if they'd known him for a long time. But he could tell they were curious. Probably wanting to ask him a million questions, most of which he couldn't answer.

Her father, of course, had given him a steady no-nonsense once-over before shaking his hand. Her twin sisters had giggled and mumbled things to each other, Anita with a shy smile and Cara with an inquisitive direct stare.

Her brother's eyes stayed hidden behind thick inky bangs. Joaquin glowered at Emmett and remained sullen and quiet while he ate the food his mother had prepared and ignored the food Belle and Emmett were sharing.

"So you two are working together?" Mr. Montera asked now, his tone level even while his dark eyes shot out an intense laser-like inspection.

"Yes, sir," they both replied at once.

Belle smiled at Emmett and then gave him a quick warning look. "A cold case that we need to clear up after a new development. And that is all we can tell you."

Gina Montera did a motherly eye roll. "Her work. Always secretive and dangerous. I worry for her, but she is brave and works hard. I'm also proud, of course."

"And you should be," Emmett said, glancing at Belle. "She's dedicated."

"Are you the one who came to her rescue?" Belle's mom asked, her dark gaze lifting and pinning Emmett.

"I did help Belle recently when someone got ornery with her while she was on her way to meet me. But she's brave and she held her own. Your daughter knows her job."

Anita's wide-eyed gaze moved from him to Belle. She looked as if she wanted to say something, but Belle tilted her chin slightly and Anita looked down at her plate.

That subtle exchange didn't get past their keen mother, but Mrs. Montera let it slip, too. It had to be hard for them, knowing Belle put herself on the line every day.

Belle's mom shifted her gaze to her daughter. "Then I thank you for coming to her aid and I am proud that she is able to handle herself out there."

Mr. Montera's frown deepened as he looked from Belle to his wife. "Belle, you are safe, right?"

"The man just told us she can take care of herself," Mrs. Montera said, patting his cheek. "You look tired. Want some ice cream?"

"Maybe later," her dad replied, his gaze on Belle. "I have to leave soon for my management meeting with one of the supers"

"Ah, *sí*."

Soon, dinner was over, Mr. Montera had left for his meeting and the girls cleared the table.

"I'll wrap up the leftovers for you," Belle's mom said.

"No. You should keep those," Emmett replied. "I did crash your meal."

"Nonsense. You are welcome here anytime."

Joaquin pushed through the kitchen. "I'm going out."

"No, you're not," Mrs. Montera said. "Just because your father had to leave doesn't mean you get to roam the streets, especially now when your sister has warned us about the man who attacked her."

Joaquin's frown shouted teenage defiance. "My friends are waiting."

Belle touched her brother's arm. "You know we're being extra careful right now. Why don't you hang around? You can come down to my place and we'll play a video game."

Joaquin tossed his bangs and rolled his eyes. "I want to go out."

"No, Joaquin," Belle said. "Not tonight."

"You can't boss me around, Belle."

"I can and I will if it means protecting you," Belle said, sending her mother a worried glance.

"I don't need your protection," her brother shouted before heading up to his room. "I know how to take care of myself."

"I'm sorry," Mrs. Montera said to Belle and Emmett. "He has a very bad attitude these days."

"Teenagers," Emmett said, trying to lighten the tension. But the danger out there was real.

When they were back down in Belle's apartment, he watched her putting away food and then turned to face her. "I guess I should head home."

"No," she said too quickly. "We didn't get a chance to talk. I need to tell you something."

"Oh, okay then, I can stay for a while."

He didn't want to leave, anyway. His place was lonely and too sterile without a woman's touch. Belle's apartment was homey and full of color and flowers. Kind of like her personality.

He should leave. Like now. And he needed to remember how this was a bad idea on so many levels, the first being he might have to help her put Randall away. After that, their heavy work schedules could ruin a good friendship.

She offered him a mineral water over ice and then poured herself one, too. "We can sit out back. I'm sure Justice could use one more break before bedtime."

They went out on the tiny stoop. Belle motioned to a folding chair off the porch and Emmett grabbed it and opened it so he could sit next to a bright red table with glass tiles covering the round top. Belle sat in her comfortable chair. Justice took off to the far corner where a gate to the alley completed a solid wooden fence that enclosed the rectangular yard.

"Nice out here," he said, enjoying the coolness of the summer evening while he scanned the yard several times. "This heat wave has everyone frazzled."

"Yes. New York in summer. Brings out the worst in people."

"Sure does." Emmett leaned in, ready to get down to business. "What did you need to tell me?"

Belle glanced up, then said on a low voice, "My sister Anita told me this earlier." She went on to explain about a man coming into the café where Anita and Cara worked for their Uncle Rico.

"He's taunting my family, Emmett. I've warned all of them and I called Gavin to ask for more protection. My Uncle Rico is aware and my dad is being diligent, too. But is it enough? Noelle and I were shot at again today."

Emmett didn't like this latest news. He wouldn't overreact, however. Belle knew her work, so he had to stay neutral even if apprehension seared through him. "I'll help you in any way, you know that."

"I'll go over his background and see what else I can find—check out gyms around his apartment and go back and confront his cagey landlord once again. Johnson's got it in for me and it goes deeper than my catching him assaulting a woman."

"Hatred like that is dangerous," Emmett warned. "He probably blames you for sending him to jail and ruining his life, but he did that all on his own. Just be careful."

"I'm going to set up camp near his apartment," Belle said. "He's got to show up sooner or later."

"I'll go with you."

"You don't need to do that."

Before she could dispute him, Justice stopped near the back gate and growled low.

Emmett held a hand on Belle's arm as they both became alert.

Belle nodded. "Let's see if anyone tries to get through that gate." She stood. "Got to get to my weapon."

Justice growled again as the gate started shaking.

Emmett stood and moved away from his chair. In the next second, something heavy came barreling down from the rooftop three floors up and landed in the chair where he'd been sitting. The chair's webbing ribbed apart.

The chunky piece of concrete had gone through the flimsy webbing and landed on one of the stone steps with a loud crack that sounded over the neighborhood.

Justice started barking now, his eyes still on the gate.

The pressure on the gate ended as Belle rushed forward. Emmett heard footsteps running away. Belle called Justice back and then reached for her cell to call for backup.

"Are you all right?" Belle said to Emmett after she got off the phone. "That could have hit you."

"Yeah, if I'd still been sitting there, it would have knocked me out." Looking toward the gate, he frowned. "Two of them?"

"The roof," she said, whirling to hurry toward the fire escape on the side of the building. "One at the gate and one on the roof."

"I'll take the fire escape," Emmett said. "You know the stairs inside better."

"I'll grab my gun on the way."

Belle took off, Justice leading the way. Emmett hurried up the rickety fire escape, worried that Belle would run headlong into a would-be killer. But she was capable, and she had Justice. He had to remind himself she'd been at her job long before he came into the picture.

He made the rooftop at about the same time she came bursting through the door. Justice bounded out with her and ran to the far corners but returned and stood at her feet.

After scanning the entire roof, she threw up her hands in frustration. "Impossible. How did they get away?"

Emmett glanced around. The roof was empty. "Is there another way into the building from here?"

"No. Just this door to the inside and up the fire escape. This door is usually locked, and we were right there by the fire escape."

"So they had someone distract us with the gate rattling and then came in through the front?" Emmett examined the heavy door to the roof. "This lock is intact."

"They had to have had access to the key at the front door," Belle said, her eyes going wide. "Emmett, that means they can enter this building anytime they want."

"That or someone you know let them in," he said, his tone grim.

"But my family members are the only ones who know about the key and where we keep it."

"Your immediate family or extended family, too?"

"My mom's sister and my dad's brothers might be aware," she said. "I'll have to ask around."

The door pushed back and her mother stood there, staring at them. "Belle, want to tell me what's going on? I heard a loud noise and then saw you flying up the stairs to the roof. Did your stalker try to get inside here?"

"Someone was here," Belle said. "I called for backup, but they're probably long gone."

Before Belle could explain what had happened, her sisters came running out onto the roof. "Joaquin is gone. He's not in his room."

An hour later, Belle and Emmett finally found her brother sitting in a park not far from their building. He was with a group of boys gathered on an old picnic table.

Justice alerted and barked, picking up her brother's scent right away.

"This is not good," Belle said, her heart dropping. "I've already had to tell my parents we might have an intruder who wants to kill me and now I might have to arrest my own brother for loitering."

"We'll handle it," Emmett told her, his eyes on the boys in the park.

Belle had to admit, it felt good knowing someone was willing to help her on all sides. She'd always had her family but Emmett saying that caused her whole system to come alive. She was beginning to really care about him. But she had to push that acknowledgment away for now.

When they pulled Emmett's big truck up to the curve, the boys all turned in surprise. Someone shouted, "Cops!"

They took off running, dropping trash on the sidewalks while they scattered in all directions.

Except for Joaquin. He stood there, glaring at her.

"Joaquin, what are you doing?" she asked, checking him over to make sure he wasn't high or hurt. Justice stood with his nose in the air.

"Having some fun," her brother said on a sneer. "Something you should try sometime."

"Hey," Emmett said, stepping in front of Belle. "You had your whole family worried. If another officer had come along, you'd all be in trouble for loitering."

Her brother looked nervous and for good reason. But that didn't stop his attitude. "Man, you can't come in here and tell me what to do."

"Yes, he can," Belle told her brother. "I'm going to give you a warning this time but next time, remember the loitering laws. This park is off-limits after dark."

Joaquin glanced around, then lowered his head.

"Yep," Emmett said. "All your buddies swarmed away. Left you having to explain things."

"They were scared," Joaquin said in a weak defense. "I'm the one who told them the cops were here."

"They were cowards," Belle retorted. "You can't keep doing this. It will only lead to trouble. They'll leave you holding the bag and I don't want it to be a bag of drugs." Reaching out, she touched his arm. "Because I won't be able to protect you if that happens."

Sullen, Joaquin looked out from underneath his bangs. He almost said something, but then clamped his mouth shut. "Can I go home now?"

"Good idea," Belle said. Then she wrapped her arm across her brother's shoulder. "Did any of those boys have drugs on them?"

"I can't say," Joaquin replied. "Okay? Just let it go."

"For now," Belle said, her voice low. "I won't tell Papá but if you mess up again, I'll have to let him know. Especially since I've warned all of you about a suspect who has it in for me—and my family."

Emmett remained silent, letting her take the lead. Another thing she liked about him. He wanted to protect her, but he also gave her the space to do her job and handle things on her own. Completely the opposite of her ex.

After they got back to her place, she turned to Joaquin. "We had an incident here tonight. Someone managed to get on our roof and drop a chunk of broken concrete down near where Emmett and I were sitting on my back stoop. Mamá and Papá and the girls are all okay. What time did you leave?"

Her brother stared up at the house. "I don't remember."

Belle sent Emmett a glance, then turned in her seat. "What do you mean? You don't know what time you snuck out?"

"I didn't look at a clock."

Shaking her head, she asked, "Did you notice anyone hanging around when you left? Did you make sure the front door was closed tight?"

Joaquin slapped at the back of her seat, his eyes downcast, causing Justice to yelp at him. "Let me out. I don't know anything about any of that."

Belle got out and let the seat down so her brother could scoot out of the jump seat. Joaquin hurried toward the house.

She stood there, watching, and then turned to Emmett. "My brother is not telling me the truth."

"Nope." Emmett glimpsed toward the house. "I think he might know something about what happened here tonight."

"Me, too," she said. "And it'll be up to me to find out what."

ELEVEN

Belle hadn't confronted Joaquin last night. When she'd gotten back inside, her parents wanted to talk to her.

"Did you find him?"

"Yes," she told her mother. "He was with some boys in the park. We broke it up and brought him home."

"I'm grounding him for a month at least," her dad said. "He'll do dishwashing duties in the café and he'll help me paint and clean apartments."

"Good idea but he might give you a hard time."

"Hard work will cure that," her father admonished. "It worked for my brothers and me."

"Now about you and the man stalking you," Mamá said. "What more should we do?"

"Change the locks, for starters," Belle said. "Sarge is going to send round-the-clock patrol cars to monitor our street and the café."

"I'll keep up our watch, too," her dad replied, nodding. "I'll alert all of your uncles again and we'll escort your mother and the girls everywhere they go. I'll keep Joaquin with me."

"This is why I wanted you to be aware," Belle said. "But please don't take matters into your own hands. That will only lead to more trouble."

"We take care of our own," her father said. "But I won't make a move without letting you know first."

That was the best she would get from him. Her father wouldn't do anything violent, but he would stand his ground.

Now, she was with Emmett in her SUV, Justice in his kennel in the back. "Today, we start with the fitness centers and gyms around Canarsie," she told Emmett. "I've reported everything to Sarge so he's aware of what I'm planning."

Emmett gave her a questioning glance. The man sure looked good first thing in the morning, all fresh and woodsy smelling, that crisp, close-cut hair shimmering a dark gold.

"Exactly what are you planning?" he asked, bringing Belle out of her crush.

"You sound worried, Marshal Gage."

"I am worried. I've seen you in action."

"I told you, first these places and then we'll revisit Lance Johnson's charming building super, Albert Stein, and get the truth out of him, at least. For all we know, he's in on this with Johnson."

Emmett absorbed that and said, "So Johnson's car has been impounded for illegal parking?"

After checking traffic, she weaved in and out of lanes.

"He didn't pay so yes, his vehicle has been removed from the lot. I hope we'll get a warrant to search it since I IDed it as the car we saw the other day at the storage unit."

Emmett glanced over at her. "I can back you up on that, at least."

"His parole officer is looking for him, too. So you might get to serve him a warrant yet."

"I'd like nothing more," Emmett said, his tone grim. "In fact, I'll alert my division and ask for that assignment."

Belle knew he'd get it done. Emmett seemed to have the respect of everyone who knew him. Too bad his cousin hadn't fared so well.

"Okay, so there are three different workout places within walking distance of Johnson's apartment," she said. "Let's start with this one."

She pulled into a beat-up parking lot and squeezed the SUV into a tight space between a sports car and a big sedan. "Well, the clientele certainly drives nice vehicles."

"Not like Johnson's at all," Emmett replied. "He abandons both his home and his vehicle. He must have someone hiding him."

"And helping him to harass my family."

Belle shuddered each time she thought of that chunk of concrete coming down so close to Emmett and her.

"Here we go," she said, using her key fob to open the back door of the SUV. "Justice will make sure no one tries to bully us."

Emmett followed her into the stifling hot gym where boxing rings warred with heavy weightlifting equipment and a musty smell permeated the air. Belle showed Lance Johnson's picture to a man who said he was the manager.

"Yeah, I remember him. He came in here a lot a couple years ago. Didn't pay his monthly dues so I kicked him out. Haven't seen him since. He was a troublemaker, anyway."

"One down and two to go."

The next fitness center looked new and smelled a little better than the last one. It had a yoga room and a spin class. "Not Johnson's type," she said to Emmett.

They talked to a woman who wore a zip-up lightweight jacket and matching workout leggings, her gym shoes designer status. "I've never seen that man in here," she said with her nose in the air. Then she checked the books. "No record of him, either."

When they were back outside, Belle said, "Okay, one more."

Belle drove about three blocks past Johnson's apartment building and pulled around the back of an old brick building that could have been a garage at one time.

They entered the big industrial doors and saw a true weightlifting arena. "We need to see the manager," she told the young man who greeted them at an old beat-up metal desk.

A burly man with a shaved head glared his way to them. "What can I do for you, officers?" he asked, giving Justice a narrow-eyed glance.

Belle pulled out the picture of Lance Johnson. "We're trying to locate this man. We think he might work out here. Do you know him?"

The man whose name tag said Perkins nodded. "Yeah, that's Lance Johnson, all right. He comes and goes and he owes me money. What kind of trouble is he into now?"

"The kind you don't want to be involved in," Emmett replied. "When was the last time he was here?"

Perkins went to the desk and pulled up a sign-in sheet. "About three weeks ago. That's the night I told him to either pay up or find another place to lift weights."

"It seems Johnson owes money to everyone we talk to," Emmett said on a droll note.

Perkins sneered in agreement.

"I'm definitely seeing a pattern," Belle replied as they

left with Perkin's assurance that if Johnson came in, he'd personally make sure to give them a call.

Next, they went to see Albert Stein for round three.

"You two again?" he asked, his jitters causing him to shuffle too many papers. "I told you, Lance Johnson skipped out on the rent he owes me and now I hear his car's been impounded. I don't know where the man is and at this point, I really don't care."

"Where's your ring, Albert?" she asked, her gaze steady on his ring finger.

"I don't know what you're talking about."

"Yes, you do." She edged closer, Justice by her side. "You see, Lance Johnson was wearing that ring the night he attacked me and I noticed you had on a similar ring when we talked the other day. Now it's not on your finger. I want to know why."

"I don't have to explain that to you," Albert replied, crossing his meaty arms over his chest in defiance.

"But you do," Belle replied. "I was here the other day with another K-9 officer. We found Johnson's car and then someone started shooting at us. You didn't seem to be on the premises. Did you fire on us, Albert?"

Albert's beady eyes widened and filled with shock. "No, I didn't fire any shots. I don't know anything about that. I was at the doctor's office all day. Gout." His expression filled with self-pity, then he turned ugly again. "You can't pin that on me. People shoot at each other in this city all the time."

"But you might have to explain a lot to a building inspector," Emmett said, pointing to the flies gathering at the overflowing trash can and a raw wire hooked up to several different electronic appliances behind the front desk.

Albert's ruddy face turned deep red but he dug in his pocket and pulled out the ring and held it up. "Okay, all right. I took the stupid ring from Johnson's apartment after he got behind on his rent. Figured it might be worth something since he liked to flash it around all the time. But the pawnbroker I took it to said it's worth about twenty-five bucks, tops. That's the honest truth."

"Why would Johnson buy this ring?" Belle wondered out loud.

"He's a show-off," Albert replied. "He likes the finer things, but he doesn't have the finesse to pull that off and he sure doesn't have the money. He's a loser."

"He's gonna be a prisoner again when I get my hands on him," Emmett replied. "You'd better let us know if he shows back up here or you'll be in a whole mess of trouble, got it?"

"I got it," Albert said. "That man has been nothing but a pain in my neck."

Belle lifted her chin. "I need that ring for evidence."

"It's mine," Albert whined.

"It's stolen," she reminded him after she pulled a couple of tissues out of a box on his desk.

Albert reluctantly handed over the ring. "If you people will leave me alone, I'll gladly give it to you."

"Good idea since technically you stole it and I don't want to take you in for lifting this cheap thing."

"I don't need that, either," he said, shaking his head.

"Thank you, Albert," Belle said with a smile. "And remember, you call us if Johnson shows his face around here."

Albert nodded and sank down on his rickety chair.

"I kind of feel sorry for him," Belle said after they'd

left the building. "He's obviously not in good health and he has to deal with the likes of Lance Johnson."

"He's a survivor," Emmett replied. "He'll land on his swollen ankles, trust me."

Belle glanced over at the man who'd stood by her since the night he'd helped save her life. She did trust him, which surprised her. She wasn't a paranoid, distrustful person to begin with but this job demanded that she couldn't fall for any sob stories or excuses until she'd studied all the evidence and found the truth. She trusted her coworkers, but they all had a silent code that kept them at a distance, anyway. It worked like a protective shield around all of them.

And yet, she knew anyone in her unit would stand by her same as Emmett was doing. But would he be willing to take things further than just having her back?

"Well, we've accomplished a few things today," she said later after they'd grabbed a pizza from a favorite hangout down the street from the K-9 headquarters. They strolled back to the unit, the last of the sun's heat turning toward sunset.

Belle held up her index finger. "Everyone who knows Lance Johnson has it in for him, so that and the fact that he didn't follow through with his probation officer has him hiding out. We should be able to get a warrant to search his vehicle now."

"His ring didn't amount to much, but Albert confessed all and should do the right thing now," Emmett added.

"But we still have two wanted men on the loose."

"I'm going to deepen my search for Randall," Emmett said. "I can't help but think he's around for some reason. He might have heard on the news about the current murders, which were so similar to the cold-case murders. Maybe he came back to find out what was going on."

"So you think the Emery murders were the work of a copycat—and not the same killer?"

Emmett shrugged. "I wish I knew. If my relative did commit the first murders, I sure hope he didn't come back to kill again on the twentieth anniversary."

"I don't know, either. I hate to say this, Emmett," Belle started. Motioning to a bench underneath a young oak, she sat down. Justice did the same. "But what if he came back because he's afraid someone's naming him for the McGregor murders? Regardless of whether he killed again or there's a copycat. What if he wants to tie up loose ends?"

Emmett rubbed a hand down his chin and glanced at the street. "I hate to say that, too, but yes, I have thought it. I don't know what's going on inside Randall's head but he has to be messed up. If I can find him and get him to talk, maybe it'll stop him from doing something stupid like killing again."

"But what if he's already killed again? What if he *is* responsible for these new murders?"

"Then our best shot is to prove that," Emmett replied, a tinge of anger in his words. "Not an easy task, but it's my job, Belle. You have to know I'll do what's right."

"I believe you will."

Belle dropped it for now. Her heart beat with sympathy for this good man trying to deal with a troubled relative.

"Hey, you know I'm on your side, right?" she said, aware of other officers passing by. "You can talk to me about anything."

Emmett's eyes shimmered like a blue lake. "Can I

talk to you about the way you make me feel?" he asked, his eyes on her.

Belle's pulse quickened while her body buzzed with a sweet surprise. "How do I make you feel?"

"Like I want to get to know you better," he admitted with a sheepish grin. "You're a beautiful distraction. All of this is new for me. I tend to keep to myself." Then he gave her another quick glance. "I quit dating because of work and I pledged to never date a woman in law enforcement. Too complicated and I figure I'd go full protection mode and she'd wind up resenting me."

Belle couldn't hide her surprise. "Well, that pledge explains a few things. I've been getting mixed vibes from you since we met, but I figured you were married to your work and…you'd always be hands-off." Shaking her head, she said, "You can relax, Marshal. I'm kind of hands-off right now, too. I'm still recovering from a man who tried his best to control me."

"That's the problem," he said, the sounds of traffic all around them. "I don't want to control you, Belle. I just want to be around you and that goes against my vow to stay away."

"And I threw you right into having to search for a relative who might be a killer and protecting me from a dangerous man. Not to mention my family's chaos."

"It's a beautiful chaos," he said. "I miss that." Then he shrugged. "As for the rest, yes, we need to get these cases out of the way."

"Okay," Belle said, getting that particular vibe loud and clear. He didn't want to take things further. Well, she didn't want that, either. "Glad we cleared the air."

She stood at about the same time he did and they

crashed. Emmett grabbed her to keep her steady, their eyes meeting, his hands on her arms.

Emmett tugged her close, his gaze moving over her face. "I guess we could test that theory."

"What?" She could barely breathe. Her heart fluttered away and a sweet longing stirred her soul.

Emmett kissed her right there on the street, around the corner from the front door to the precinct building. Belle should have pulled away. Too many officers coming and going, too many emotions hitting at her resistance.

But she couldn't let go.

Emmett ended the kiss way too soon. But when he stepped back, realization flared and put out the other flame between them.

"That was a mistake," he said. Then he quickly amended. "I mean, not that kissing you was a mistake. I liked that part. But I know better. I'm sorry I put you in a bad position."

Belle had to find her voice and get her brain settled. "We can't do this. Our work, the crazy hours, the cases we're working on together. Fraternizing is never a good idea. You just said that and then you kiss me?"

He glanced around and so did she. "I'm sorry, Belle. I shouldn't have."

Thankful that no one was walking by, Belle called to Justice. "I have to get back. It's late and I have reports to file."

Emmett nodded. "I should go home and book an appointment to have my head examined."

"Why? Are you sick?"

"No, but I know better."

"Emmett, this threw me." She shrugged. "I don't have

a very good record in the relationship department and you obviously don't want a relationship with anyone."

"Threw me, too, and threw my self-imposed pledge right out the window. But I liked kissing you and I want to kiss you again."

Belle wanted to allow that but hesitated. "Again, not a good idea right now. We've been thrown together on two cases and we're not thinking straight."

"So you're determined to avoid the obvious?"

"No, I'm just cautious. I like you and I owe you my life."

"Is that why you kissed me back? Because you feel obligated, filled with gratitude?"

Belle laughed and started back around the building. "I can assure you, Marshal Gage, that right there was not gratitude."

He caught up with her. "So you're saying if we went on a real date and were walking through a park, you'd let me kiss you again."

She grinned. "As long as I'm not being mauled by a criminal, yes, I'd let you kiss me again. But I'm going to have to think about this, a lot. Kissing you is one thing. But watching you walk away is another."

A fire of frustration roared across his face. "I'll see you around, then, Officer Montera."

"I'll be right here, Deputy Marshal Gage."

She watched him walk to his truck, then turned to go inside.

And ran smack into Sergeant Gavin Sutherland.

TWELVE

"Uh…hello, sir," Belle said, her skin burning red with embarrassment. Her gaze moved from Gavin to watching Emmett walk around the corner to where he'd parked his vehicle.

Gavin inclined his head and glanced to the street. "You and Gage seem to be on good terms."

Not knowing what Sarge had seen, she bobbed her head. "Yes, we get along great."

Gavin's eyebrow twitched but he didn't say anything to her about what he might have heard or seen. "Any work-related news for me?"

"We're after a warrant to search Lance Johnson's vehicle and we found the ring he was wearing." She explained about Albert Stein. "So that verifies that Johnson had to be my attacker since it was his ring that Albert swiped. I sent it to the lab to check for DNA and fibers." Tugging at her bun, she added, "With the fibers and epidermis particles the techs scraped from my fingernails, added to this new information, we're building a strong case against Johnson."

Gavin crossed his arms and pursed his lips. "That's all great, but we need to *find* your attacker."

"I'm on that, sir. He's good at hiding but we do have

people at his old hangouts watching out for him. None of them want him back, either."

Gavin scanned the area and nodded. "And Randall Gage? No one seems to be able to get a handle on him, not even a trained US marshal who happens to be his relative."

"Emmett's trying, sir. He's good at his job and I know he wants to find out the truth. He's put out feelers and asked around all over Bay Ridge and beyond."

"We need to track down and verify any leads, Belle."

"We will, sir. We're meeting up tomorrow to explore Randall's work records, if we can find any. He works for pay under the table a lot from what Emmett's dad left in his notes."

"Keep your focus."

"Yes, sir. I will. Emmett and I might be becoming friends but that's it."

"Right." Gavin's hard-edged face softened. "I remember saying that about Brianne and me, and you see where that got me."

"You two make it work somehow," Belle replied, smiling.

Gavin's usually stoic expression turned into a broad grin. "Yes, we do. In spite of the odds. With her help, I've come a long way in learning how to deal with people. She's part of why I'm here today. She believed in me when it seemed no one else did." He jingled his keys. "Speaking of that, I'm going to go get Tommy from the groomer and then I'm going home to my wife."

"Have a good night, sir," Belle said, Gavin's words buzzing in her head. She believed in Emmett even when some on the team didn't trust him. She couldn't blame Bradley or even Penny for having doubts. Emmett reminded them of the man who could have possibly killed their parents.

Whirling, she took Justice and headed to the reception desk. "Hi, Penny," she said. "Can I ask you something regarding your parents' case?"

Twenty-four-year-old Penny's brown eyes took on the guarded wariness everyone around here was used to seeing. "I guess." Her freckles looked more pronounced when she got anxious, Belle noticed.

"I know you've been asked this over and over, but I was wondering if you can go over with me what you remember about the man who murdered your parents."

Penny shifted in her chair. Her mouth set in a firm line tightened and her brow puckered. "He had on that horrible clown mask with blue hair. But…his eyes. I can't say for sure what color they were—maybe greenish—but if I ever saw him again, I think I'd know him by his eyes."

This was all in the file, of course, and Penny had answered these questions many times the past few months since the second murders. But Belle kept hoping Penny might suddenly remember something, anything. "Okay. Maybe his eyes struck for a reason. Did you ever think you might have seen him someplace else?"

Penelope shrugged. "Bradley used to pick me up at the day care. I guess he could have been someone who dropped off his own kids there, if he even had kids. I don't remember much but…he had to have known my parents. Why else target them? Why else leave me alive and well? And give me a toy?"

Belle nodded sympathetically. "What was the name of the day care?"

"Happy Day. No. Happy Child," Penelope replied. "Although I don't remember being very happy there. I always wanted to be home with my parents." Then Penny stopped, her lips twisting. "I've answered a lot of questions, but I've blocked most of that time. I think there might have been a man who always brought toys to us."

Belle halted, remembering the picture Emmett had found of Randall as a little boy holding a stuffed dog. "What else do you remember? Can you describe the man?"

Penelope shook her head. "No. I mostly noticed the cute little stuffed animals," Penelope said. "Whoever killed my parents gave me a little monkey wrapped in plastic. I don't like monkeys very much now."

Belle found the picture of Randall she'd sent to Gavin that first night. It was a longshot; Penny had been only four years old then. "Does this look like the man from the day care?"

Penny studied the picture, her expression darkening. "I can't be sure. It's been so long."

"Thanks, Penny," Belle said, wishing her friend didn't have to go through this again. What a nightmare.

Belle and Justice headed home. Tired but alert, Belle kept an eye on the rearview mirror and thought about Emmett, her brother and her family. Then she thought about Bradley and Penny and what they'd been through. She prayed for all of them.

"Father, take care of the people I love. And please help Emmett get through this."

Justice listened to her spoken prayers and woofed an Amen.

She loved her partner so much.

Why couldn't humans be so easy to love?

When she got home, her sisters were sitting on the inside stairs, waiting for her.

"Belle, we need to talk," Cara said. "Inside your apartment."

"Okay." Cara looked so serious. Belle's heart rate increased tenfold. "Is everything okay?"

Anita shut the door and nodded at her sister. "Tell her."

Cara twisted her braid and said, "When Uncle Rico brought us home today, we saw Joaquin talking to a man. It looked like the man gave him a wad of money."

Belle froze, her heart dropping like a brick. "Where was this?"

Cara scuffed her pink sneakers against the wooden floor. "Near the old park down the way where you found him the other night."

"Did Uncle Rico see him?"

"No," Anita said. "I poked Anita and we both watched him but didn't say anything." Shrugging, she looked up at Belle. "We decided to tell you first."

"You did the right thing," Belle replied, her mind spinning ahead. "What did the man look like?"

"Like the one you described." Anita pushed at her long hair. "The same man who came into the café the other day."

Belle tried to keep the panic out of her voice. "Text me when Joaquin gets home. I want to talk to him."

"Don't tell him we said anything," Cara said in a low voice. "He gets really mad when we mess with him."

"Well, he can get over that," Belle said as she fed Justice and gave him fresh water before letting him out back. "I won't say who told me, though."

"Oh, and there's one more thing," Anita said. "The man got into a car that we think we recognized."

"What kind of car?"

"One like your ex Percy used to drive. Black. An old BMW."

Belle's heart did flip-flops and her whole system went still again. "Are you telling me that the man who tried to choke me to death got in a car with Percy Carolo?"

"It looked like Percy," Cara told her. "It happened fast while we were stopped at the traffic light by the park so we could be wrong."

Belle motioned to her sisters and took them into her arms. "You did good. This is very important information. Don't mention this to Mamá and Papá, okay? I'll talk to them in private. Joaquin could run away if he thinks we suspect him."

"We won't," Cara said, her hand reaching up to push Belle's falling hair out of her eyes. "What do you think he's doing with that man?"

"I don't know," Belle said. "But you don't need to worry. I have a lot of people watching out for us and Justice will protect this whole house."

She kissed her sisters and sent them upstairs. "I'll be up for dinner after I freshen up."

She almost called Emmett after they left but she needed to process this. Why would Joaquin be taking money from Lance Johnson? And why would Johnson have any reason to be hanging out with her vindictive, bitter ex-boyfriend?

At a tense dinner where Joaquin picked at his food and ignored everyone, Belle tried to keep the conversation flowing while she prayed the whole time that her sisters wouldn't blurt something out. Her mother watched all of them with a hawk eye but remained quiet. She'd probably question the twins and Belle later. After helping with the dishes, Belle came back to her apartment and immediately did a background check on Percy Carolo.

They'd met years ago at the police academy and had hit it off instantly. Percy was one of those beautiful men who had a lot of charm but no substance. Belle had realized that too late, however. They'd had to be careful while in training, but they'd dated and things became serious pretty quickly. When graduation time came, things took a turn for the worst.

Belle had passed with flying colors but Percy had failed due to a bad attitude and a constant fight with authority.

"I can't believe this," Percy had said by way of congratulating her. "You get through and leave me in the dirt?"

"Percy, we both had the same training. You know how hard I worked for this."

"What about me, Belle? I worked hard and still got shot down at every turn. It's not fair. I'm every bit as qualified as you."

"Of course you are," she'd replied, hoping to soothe him.

But Percy couldn't be soothed, and he didn't have the grace to be happy for her.

He hadn't taken things very well at the time, but because she'd seen his good side when they'd first started dating, Belle believed she could make it work despite how he'd started trying to undermine her and manipulate her. She went on to become a rookie officer while he got odd jobs here and there and finally wound up in security.

But he was never happy being a mall cop or a night watchman and claimed he would have been better at her job than she was. Which made no sense. He had no patience with humans or animals and scorned all of his superiors and coworkers. A lot of talk and no real action.

She'd ended the bad romance when they'd gotten into a fight on the day she should have been celebrating getting on with the Brooklyn K-9 Unit. Angry and jealous, he'd come at her and almost hit her. Taking him down and knocking him flat on his back hadn't helped matters.

That ended her long run with a confused, abusive, hotheaded man who'd almost ruined her self-confidence and could have cost her a career if she'd stayed with him. Being with Percy had made her distrustful toward other men.

That's why she'd held back with Emmett. But Emmett wasn't anything like Percy. Emmett was confident and brave and went beyond the call of duty. He knew his job well and he got along with just about everyone. He just didn't want to commit to anyone. Especially someone like her.

Belle couldn't consider anything beyond friendship until she was out from under this cloud of fear for her family and for herself. Emmett obviously didn't need her in his life. He had to find his cousin. Emmett was closed off and shuttered, maybe because he'd lost both his parents and his grief had hardened his heart. He lived for his work. Period.

Remembering their kiss, Belle tried to clear her head and get back to business.

Now she wondered if Percy had been keeping tabs on her since the day they'd broken up. She hadn't seen Percy since she'd left his apartment that night. Where had he been for the past two years?

After searching for over an hour, Belle knew exactly where Percy had been. More odd jobs and short stints at various places around Brooklyn. The man couldn't hold down a job.

Then she found something that set her hair on edge and made her pulse burn.

Percy Carolo was currently employed as a security guard at City Wide Storage. The very storage unit where someone had shot at Belle and Emmett a few days ago.

Her stomach roiling, Belle stared at her laptop screen and wondered if her ex had somehow teamed up with Lance Johnson to harass her and her family. How could that even be possible?

What were the odds?

Then she reminded herself that while she lived in a big city, small neighborhoods had their own grapevines and ways of communicating. Anything was possible.

Unable to sleep, she made notes and set up a timeline to see if she could match a cross section between Percy and Lance Johnson. They could have easily moved in the same circles—the gym, piecemeal work habits, bars where angry bitter men hung out and picked fights with each other. Somehow, she had to find a way to connect them.

And she would definitely plan to do a little surveillance at the park up the street. Because now, they'd possibly gotten her baby brother involved and there was no way on earth she would let Joaquin go down that road.

Not without a fight, anyway.

THIRTEEN

Emmett walked into the 646 Diner and searched among the many NYPD uniforms to find Belle in a corner booth with Justice lying at her feet.

All around, officers sat in clusters in the old booths and chunky tables enjoying the greasy-spoon menu, laughing and discussing life. Some of them noticed him and waved since he'd somehow become a fixture around these parts lately.

Maybe he'd get his photo up on the wall, too, he thought with a wry twist.

"Hey," he said as he settled down across from Belle in the booth and removed his dark cap. "What's up? Your message sounded kind of frantic."

"I am frantic," Belle admitted, her pretty eyes dark with apprehension. She told him about her sisters seeing Joaquin taking money from a man in the park. "They said the man looked like Lance Johnson, the same man Anita saw in my uncle's café."

"Okay, so why would he give your brother money?"

"That's the question," Belle said, staring at her half-eaten eggs and toast. "I didn't get to corner Joaquin last night, but I explained what was going on to my parents.

We're all on edge. The girls and I were tense and worried at dinner and Joaquin barely ate."

Emmett didn't like the sound of this. "The boy's in trouble, Belle. We need to question him."

"I am, today, somehow." She lowered her head and then whispered, "There's more. The girls saw Lance Johnson get in a car with someone I know."

"Okay? Who?"

"My ex-boyfriend Percy Carolo."

"Your ex?" Emmett touched a hand to his coffee cup. "You've never talked about him much."

"And for good reason. The man messed with my head and tried to mess with my career. He didn't take it well when we got in a fight about my making it in law enforcement when he couldn't. He came at me and I dropped him on his back."

A heat flared in Emmett's gut. "Did he abuse you?"

Belle glanced away and then back to him. "He tried. Not so much physically but he tried to undermine me and make me feel bad about myself, whined at me for getting a promotion and constantly implied he would do better at my job than I ever could."

"Did he also work for the force?"

She shook her head. "No. We met in the academy and trained together but he flunked out and had to settle for pick-up work here and there—security mostly. From what I've gathered, he subs a lot in security and works crowd control at big events, whatever he can find."

"Okay, so why would he be with Lance Johnson?"

Belle sat still, her eyes holding Emmett's. She couldn't seem to bring herself to say the words.

So Emmett did it for her. "You think those two have partnered up to attack you and harm your family, Belle?"

"It looks that way," she said, letting out a breath. Then she told him what they'd found out so far. "If Percy's involved, he'll play Lance Johnson like a fiddle and have the man doing his bidding. And if he's got my little brother involved, I'll go after both of them and make them pay dearly."

Emmett touched his hand on hers in a brief display of assurance. "Steady. Don't go rogue here. We do this by the book, and we'll bring 'em both in. Together."

"You shouldn't have to deal with this, Emmett. You've got enough just trying to find Randall."

"I'm in it," he said, his tone firm. "I'm in it for you and I won't leave you on your own. This is dangerous."

"Well, there's one more piece to the puzzle," she said, her wary expression showing the stress of the last few days. "Percy works at the City Wide Storage warehouse where you keep your parents' stuff."

Emmett let out a breath. "Are you kidding me?"

"I wish. He's either been watching me and saw me there with you or…he saw us and called Lance to come and do us in. I don't know yet. But…I'm going to find out."

"*We're* going to find out," Emmett corrected. "Don't do this without me."

She nodded, gratitude in her eyes. "Thank you, Emmett."

He gazed over at her, his own concerns deepening and turning stormy. "Belle, what's going on with us?"

"I don't know," she admitted. "But one day, when this is all behind us, maybe we can figure that out together."

"If you can trust me," he said. "This Percy left you in a mess, didn't he?"

"He did. I haven't dated much since him because I love my work and some men just can't handle that."

"I'm not one of those men," he said. "I admire you and see you as a valuable part of the NYPD. Don't you ever forget that."

"You're a good man, Emmett."

"Don't forget that either, then," he said, giving her what looked like a genuine smile. "Now, let's get to work."

Both of their phones buzzed as if on cue.

Belle answered hers first. "Belle, it's Lani."

"Hi, Lani," Belle said. She liked Lani Jameson even though some thought she got special treatment because she was married to a chief from another K-9 unit. But Lani had joined *their* team to avoid any conflicts and worked hard to prove herself. Sometimes Belle got together with Lani and Noelle for girl talk. "What's up?"

"We could use your help," Lani replied. "We've tracked a stray dog who recently had pups to an old two-family brick home not far from the precinct. She's under the house with her puppies and we're trying to lure her out since we heard the house has been condemned. I thought you might be able to help since you're so good with soothing the dogs when they're in training."

Belle thought of all the things she needed to be working on but she couldn't turn down Lani or a hurting animal. "We'll be there in fifteen minutes," she said. "Emmett Gage is with me."

"Oh, okay," Lani replied. "So you and Emmett—seeing a lot of each other these days?"

"Working on a case, as I've said," Belle reminded Lani, lifting her gaze to where Emmett stood, taking his own call. She could just picture Lani's blue eyes going bright with interest. "For now."

"Okay, we'll talk later," Lani said. "Thanks, Belle."

Belle ended the call and took one last sip of coffee. Dropping some bills on the table, she motioned to Justice and they met up with Emmett at the front door.

After explaining that Lani needed some help, she asked, "Do you want to come with me? We can work on these new developments after we see about this stray dog."

"Yes," he said. "I told you I'm in this. Unless I get called away, I'm going to shadow you as often as I can." Then he added, "And that call I got? A friend on the force thinks he spotted Randall at a diner near where he used to live. Couldn't be sure it was him since it's been a while since my friend has seen Randall, but I'm going to case the place and see if he shows up again. My source said he was there earlier. Goes there a lot for coffee, if it's him, that is."

Surprised, Belle said, "Should you go?"

"No, Randall's not there now. My source confirmed that. I can help you today. But tomorrow morning, I'll be at that old diner and let's hope I see Randall there."

"Meantime, I'll let Sarge know," she said as they loaded up Justice and headed toward the street Lani had named. "He can put someone on the diner, too, for now."

"Yeah, he'd want to know," Emmett said on a gritty note. "No reason to give him anything else to chew on while he wonders if he can trust me or not."

"We all trust you, Emmett. It's just that trust comes hard when you're dealing with murder and mayhem."

"Yeah, well, we both have that problem," he replied.

But the look in his eyes told her he wanted her to know he was dependable.

Belle believed that, at least. She could depend on Emmett to finish what he'd started. But she couldn't trust him to start something with her and then not break it off when he decided he couldn't handle it.

The noonday heat beat down on them like falling embers, but Emmett was determined to get this dog and her pups out from under this collapsing house. He had a lot to think about and he'd rather be casing the neighborhood where his cousin might possibly be but he'd promised Belle he'd help with this stray and her little family. Only it was taking longer than they'd planned.

"Got any more ideas?" he asked Belle after an hour of sweating and calling and offering treats to the scared, scrawny German shepherd.

Lani told them she'd named the mama dog Brooke, short for Brooklyn, and that best she could tell from shining a light down in the hole was that five puppies were with Brooke. They could hear the furry puppies yelping and crying out where they were embedded in the deep hole their mama must have dug to protect them.

Belle refused to leave them there.

"It's supposed to storm later," she told Emmett. "Look at the sky. Dark. They'll get wet when the water comes down from the roof."

"Well, we're running out of ideas," he said as he belly-crawled as close to the dogs as he could get. "If I get stuck, you'll have to ply me with treats, too."

Belle laughed at that. She looked adorable with her hair falling down and dirt on her sweaty nose. Her love for animals showed in her concern for these little ones and their mother.

That kind of commitment made Emmett want to be around her even more. She surprised him on a daily basis, something his jaded mind couldn't comprehend. But their conversation last night had set a new pace between them, one that kept things on a professional level. But then he'd gone and kissed her, which had blown away his theory of not getting involved.

"How about we put some dry food in water and soften it?" she said, causing him to come back to the present. "Maybe she's too weak to eat a chew treat."

"Whatever might work," he replied. Like everything else involving her, Emmett was beginning to go all in.

Belle went to her SUV and got water and a bowl. Justice followed back and forth with his eyes but remained sitting where she told him. She didn't want her partner to scare the frightened mama dog. But Justice was trained to stay on task, so he took it all in with wide eyes and perked up ears.

After she'd soaked the kibbles, Belle slowly slid the bowl close to the tight opening under the crooked porch, brushing at spiderwebs and old wasp nests.

"C'mon, Brooke. Sweet girl, let us help you," Belle said, her voice soft and reassuring. "We'll take you and your babies to a safe place where you can all thrive." Smiling, she kept cooing and speaking in a calm voice. "I think your little fluffy balls of fur can be trained to become some of the best of the best. What do you think? Your five cuties becoming NYPD K-9s? Pretty impressive, huh?"

"They do look like full-blooded shepherds," Emmett noted. "You might be right on that, Belle."

"We think so," Lani added. "Just need to get them in and let Doc Mazelli have a look."

Behind her and Emmett, Lani stood trying to do her best to help, her blond messy bun even messier now. "Belle, do you want me to take over?"

"Nope. Let her get used to me," Belle said. "Just keep Justice happy so he doesn't scare her."

Lani called to Justice and ruffled his fur. Her K-9 partner, Snapper, was nearby so she ordered Justice to stand with him. Belle's partner seemed to take it all in stride. Emmett wished he could.

"She's moving toward the bowl," Belle said, handing him a short leash. "Emmett, as soon as she eats a bite or two, you'll have to throw this leash like a lasso and hold her by her fur and tug her out so we can get her in a kennel."

"I'm ready," Emmett said, amazed at Belle's dedication.

The mama dog finally took the bait and dove toward the waiting food. Belle let her eat several bites while she kept petting the hungry mama on the head and reassuring her. Then she moved the dish closer to the opening, allowing Emmett a chance to grab the dog and drag her out.

Emmett was careful to be gentle as he roped the soft fabric across the dog's head and tugged on her middle. She growled and tried to nip at him, but he held her steady. "Got her."

He passed the yelping dog off to Lani and Noelle, who got her into a kennel and gave her more water, all the while talking to her in soothing voices.

Belle went in and grabbed the first of the puppies and soon they had all of them out, one by one, until all five were accounted for. They were dirty and skinny but still alive, their big black eyes bright with fear.

By the time they'd finished up and had the puppies in a separate kennel in Lani's vehicle, the sky had turned dark and big drops of rain hit their sweaty faces.

"Thank you for helping," Belle said once they were

headed back to the precinct. "I need a good shower and I'm sure you want to get on with your day."

Emmett glanced over at her, his mind in turmoil with protecting her and needing to hunt down his cousin. "I do. You need to follow up on the connection between Lance Johnson and your ex."

"Yes, that I will do."

"I'm going home to get cleaned up," Emmett said, watching as Lani and Noelle took Brooke and her puppies to the training center, where the vet would give them all examinations and clean them up. "Then I'm going to swing by the diner where my friend thought he saw Randall. How about I check back with you later and we can compare notes?"

"Okay," Belle said. "I'll be here, catching up on paperwork and calling around to find out what's up with my ex and Lance Johnson. They had to have run into each other somewhere. I need to prove they've been seen together recently beyond what my sisters told me."

"You'll be careful, right?" Emmett asked. "Don't go out alone. Take a buddy if I'm not back."

Belle shook her head. "You tend to forget what I do for a living, Marshal." Then she put her hands on her hips. "Let me rephrase that. You know exactly what I do for a living."

"Yes," he replied. "I haven't forgotten that for a moment since I met you." And now that she knew how he felt about things, she wouldn't forget it, either.

She slanted her eyes at him as she bent her head to one side. "I get it now. We met under unusual circumstances and now we're forced together until this ends. At least I know where I stand with you."

"Nope, you have no clue where you stand with me, Belle."

Emmett left the building, well aware that Belle's co-workers were watching him like a hawk. If he didn't produce something soon on Randall's whereabouts, he might get asked to leave and never return. He was in too deep with Belle even after he'd tried to explain his stance.

He and Belle might not have a chance to finish what they'd started on a personal level. He should have been glad about that.

Since he didn't plan on letting her go despite his stupid pledge, he decided he'd work double time to solve both of these cases.

And he'd stay close to Belle, no matter the outcome.

FOURTEEN

After Belle reported what her sisters had seen to Gavin, he suggested she stay put for today. "I'll send someone else to ask around about your ex. Makes sense he might have hung around the same locations as Johnson and somehow, they started comparing notes."

Belle wondered how, then a thought dropped into her brain. "This case, sir. The cold case."

"What's that got to do with this?" Gavin asked.

"It was all over the news, in all the local papers. We were on the news when the second set of murders happened. That's probably how Lance found me again. If he was in a place with Percy, and the news report was on television, they could have compared notes again."

Gavin nodded. "And not in a good way."

"No, sir. They both have grudges against me."

"Okay, you stay here. I'm sending someone to the storage warehouse and back to the gyms and bars around Johnson's neighborhood. Let's pull up a photo of both of them so they can show them around."

Belle did as he asked, glad she could do her own checks and wait here for Emmett. Sarge was right. She'd been seen and recognized and now it was even more dangerous for her family.

She still had to talk to Joaquin, too. That would be the hardest part. But her sisters had reported that he was working with Papá today.

So she sat at her desk while Justice got in some practice with a handler in the training center. Going back over her time with Percy was like opening a jagged wound but Belle had changed and grown since then. No man would ever intimidate her again.

She thought of Emmett and how he'd helped her and Lani and Noelle today. He hadn't complained much at all and he'd done his part in bringing Brooke and her pups to safety. Maybe they could name one of the pups after Emmett. Why did she want to be with him even when she was afraid to even try?

That made her smile.

He made her smile.

"You're smiling."

She looked up to find Brianne Hayes-Sutherland giving her an amused look. "Hi, Brianne," she said, getting up to hug Gavin's wife. "How are you?"

"I'm good," Brianne said, her face splitting in a grin. "I'm supposed to be having lunch with my husband."

"He's in his office," Belle said. "But Penny probably already told you that."

"She did." Brianne shrugged. "It's my day off so I'm stealing him for an hour or so."

"Good plan," Belle said, noting Brianne's street clothes and loose hair. "How's Miss Stella?"

"Stella is amazing," Brianne said, referring to her partner, a yellow Lab trained in bomb detection. Stella had been gifted to them pregnant, and Liberty, Noelle's partner, was one of her now-grown pups. "Has the best instincts. I love working with her but lately, things have been quiet for us. Thankfully."

They chatted a few more minutes, then Gavin came out and kissed his wife. "I need to talk to Belle a minute and then I'm yours for the next hour or so."

"I like that," Brianne said, her dark eyes sparkling.

After she moved on to visit with other officers, Gavin turned to Belle. "One of the officers I sent out said the gym owner you and Emmett talked to the other day recognized the photo of your ex. Said he came in with Johnson a few weeks ago."

Belle's stomach lurched as if she'd eaten something that had gone bad. Her skin became clammy and heated. "Then they do know each other."

"Yes," Gavin said. "He remembered snippets of their trash talk. Seems they met when Percy Carolo worked as a guard on a short stint at Rikers Island Prison. A very short stint from what I found after I verified that."

Belle's whole system buzzed, concern for her family and everyone she knew gnawing at her. "So they might have gotten to know each other there."

"Yes. Seems that's a good start. Carolo got fired after only a couple of weeks—for being a hothead and for associating with the inmates a little too much."

"I can attest to the hothead part," Belle said. "Apparently, that hasn't improved since I left him. I think he belongs on the other side of those bars now."

Gavin gave her a serious look, his brow puckering. "This is getting more and more dangerous. With two of them against you, you're not safe anywhere."

"I just want my family safe," she said. "I need to find my brother and get him to talk to me."

"Not alone," Gavin replied. "Get someone to go with you or call Emmett back in if that makes you feel better."

She stared at him in surprise. "Yes, sir. We're supposed to meet up later to see if he spotted his cousin at the diner where he might have been seen this morning."

"As long as you have a partner," he said. "Now if I don't get Brianne out of here, I'm going to be in the kennel with Tommy and Stella tonight."

Belle nodded at that and watched as they walked away, laughing with each other. They were really in love.

When she looked up from the computer an hour later, Emmett was walking toward her in plain clothes. "I thought I'd check in."

Her frustrations regarding this new development lifted like a mist. "Yes. I have an update on my situation."

He listened as they headed to get Justice.

"Gage, why don't you just apply and become a K-9 officer with us?" K-9 Detective Henry Roarke asked, his brown eyes full of a knowing gleam. "You're in here about as much as I am these days."

Henry was on modified duty due to a pending investigation regarding him possibly using excessive force when dealing with a twenty-year-old suspect. So he'd been stuck here filing papers, answering the phone and doing some training with the K-9s, waiting for internal affairs to send in a new investigator. The last one had recently had a heart attack.

Emmett grinned and shook Henry's hand. "I just might do that before it's all over. This is not a bad place to hang out."

"You'd change that tune if you had to deal with what I'm dealing with." Henry shot Belle a wry smile, shook his head and kept moving. Belle and he were good friends so he liked to rag on her about her love life. He'd been down lately so she tried to visit with him when she could.

"He's going through a lot right now," Belle told Emmett as they were leaving. She'd explained to him about Henry when she'd first introduced them. Now Henry kept a keen eye on her and Emmett.

Emmett's silvery gaze moved over her face. "You all seem close. I like that."

"How about you and your people?"

"Oh, we get along and work hard but we're so scattered and always on the go. Hard to get too intimate." Shrugging, he said, "Hard to get close to anyone."

Belle heard that as, yet again, a warning to her. Was he really going to deny that kiss and how he felt for her? Well, she'd denied it over and over, so could she blame him?

"And that's the thing," she replied. "The work comes first and right now I have a lot to accomplish."

He gave her an understanding glance, a dark longing in his eyes. "Agreed. So what's the plan?"

"I want to see if I can talk to Joaquin before I do anything else. He was asleep when I left this morning and my dad had plans for him to help paint apartments all day. He's supposed to stay at home tonight."

She glanced at her watch. "It's still early so I should catch him when they come home around four or so."

"Okay. Meanwhile, I'll catch up on some paperwork."

"Sorry you came by. You could have called."

"Maybe I wanted to see you."

"Why, Emmett?" she asked, wishing he'd really open up to her.

"I don't like how we left things last night."

Belle shook her head. "Oh, you mean that kiss, after

you'd told me in no uncertain terms that you have a stead-fast aversion to dating anyone, especially another law enforcement person. This kind of work and all of that?"

"Yeah, that."

"I'll check in with you later," she replied, determined to stay on track.

"Belle?"

She whirled to face him. "What?"

"Never mind. Just be safe, okay?"

Belle headed home, anxiety for her brother front and center in her mind. But getting used to having a man like Emmett around sure was tempting. After Percy, she'd concentrated on work and hanging out with her family and friends. Emmett made her realize that might not be enough. Funny, he'd made her see that but he couldn't see he needed people in his life, too.

When she got home, her mother met her inside the entryway, her eyes red-rimmed, her hand clutching her blouse.

"I'm so relieved you're home early, Belle. Your brother is missing again. You have to find him."

Belle circled the park again, telling herself Joaquin had to be all right. He might have come here, but had he left with Percy and Lance?

When she saw a dark pickup, she let out a sigh of re-lief. She'd texted Emmett and he'd insisted on coming to help her. She'd also called in the patrols that had been watching her building.

"We didn't see your brother exit your house," one of the patrolmen told her. "But he could have gone out the back."

It was impossible to keep someone on him 24/7, Belle

knew. Her brother wasn't stupid. He'd probably timed the rounds the patrolmen made and managed to sneak right by one of them.

She parked her vehicle and used her key fob to open the back door for Justice to jump out. He'd be needed on this search.

"Hey," Emmett said, putting on his official cap while he scanned the deserted park. "Nothing?"

"Not yet. I have one of his shirts so I'm going to let Justice sniff it and hopefully we can locate him." She lifted her head to the dark clouds that had dumped rain off and on all day. "We have to find him."

"We will," Emmett said. "How are your parents?"

"Frantic and angry. They didn't raise him to turn into a hooligan."

"He's not there yet, but things could go bad if he's listening to that duo harassing you."

"That's the part that driving me nuts," she admitted. "I brought this on my family, Emmett."

"Hey, now, you were doing your job and you also were wise to dump Percy. Don't beat yourself up. These two aren't wired the same way we are, Belle."

"No, they're not. That's the scary part." She lifted her gaze to meet his. "We're wired to do this and everything else is secondary."

They started walking the perimeters of the rundown park. Belle let Justice smell the shirt she'd brought and then loosened the leash so Justice could get to work.

When she saw a cluster of teens, she flagged them down and showed them a recent picture of her brother. "Have you seen him today? And don't try to bluff me. It won't work."

One of the boys gave her a confused stare, his sandy

bangs falling over his eyes. "I think I saw him maybe two hours ago, talking to two men."

Belle swallowed the bile in her throat and tried to breathe. "Did he leave with them?"

"No. They all walked that way."

The boy pointed to an overgrown area of the park by a small dark pond.

Taking Justice back out, Belle tried to focus on her training and not the horrible thoughts running rampant through her mind. The trees were heavy with humidity, the wind hot on her clammy skin. Every twig that snapped set her senses on edge.

"Hang on," Emmett said, his steady presence holding her together. "We'll find him, Belle."

His reassurances helped, but Belle's worst fears pushed her like a hot breath on her skin. What would her parents do if something had happened to their only son?

"Justice, let's go."

The big dog sniffed the air and the ground, moving slowly at times and picking up the pace at other times, his ears up and his gait full of energy. They moved on a grid back and forth, past rusted-out swing sets and crooked piping hot metal slides. A wobbly merry-go-round moved eerily in the wind, whining a forlorn moan with each circle.

The desolate undergrowth of the heavily wooded corner of the park only added to Belle's concerns. She looked for lurkers around the bushes and old trees. The swaying oaks hovered like sulking giants ready to attack. The wind hissed a hot warning that rasped at her soul. Remembering the feel of her attacker's beefy hands on her neck, she closed her eyes and prayed for her brother.

God would protect Joaquin even if Joaquin seemed to scorn God these days.

I hope he calls out to You, Lord, she prayed.

They came up on an old shack—probably used for storage. Justice held up his head, his nose in the air, his body quivering with an intensity that had Belle's hair standing on edge. Justice knew her brother's scent as well as he knew her own and all of her family's.

Belle glanced at Emmett, every fiber of her being dreading what she might discover in that shed. Bracing herself, she swallowed and breathed, determined to keep moving. Somewhere over the trees, lightning hit the tepid air. A roll of thunder boomed a shattered stomp of urgency.

"Find," she said to Justice.

The German shepherd trotted to the shed and stood at alert, a soft whine whispering through his clenched teeth. Then he turned and looked back at Belle.

A sure sign of confirmation he'd honed in on her brother's scent.

Emmett stepped forward and touched a hand to her arm. "Let me go in first, Belle."

Belle couldn't breathe, but she had to keep moving. "I'll be right behind you," she said, conceding that she really needed Emmett to help her do this.

Emmett gave her a grim nod and then silently walked toward the shed, his weapon drawn, his body coiled in a low crouch. When he pushed at the rickety metal door, it fell open with a noisy groan and several howling screeches of protest.

A dove cooed and flew off the roof of the old building, the fluttering of his wings only matching the beat of a heavy pulse hitting at Belle's temples.

Emmett stuck his head inside and looked down. Then he stepped into the darkness of the building. "Belle, he's here."

Belle rushed forward, her heart in her throat, the worst images running through her mind.

Emmett went down on his knees.

Belle's gaze followed him. Justicc leaped inside and then she spotted her brother lying still on the floor. "Joaquin, no! Joaquin?"

Emmett gently tugged at her brother and rolled him over. He groaned and blinked, his gaze unfocused and dull.

"Hey, Belle," Joaquin said, his eyes bruised and swollen, his lip bleeding. "I guess I'm in big trouble, huh?"

Belle fell down beside him. "Joaquin." Then she took him in her arms and hugged him tight, tears burning at her eyes. "Yes, you are so in trouble. But…I love you. Always, I love you."

FIFTEEN

Belle paced outside the hospital room, her mind roiling between anger and fear. Her parents were in with Joaquin. Once they could see that he was okay despite the many bruises and cuts on his face and body, she'd go in and get the truth out of him.

Pushing at the bun she'd long ago forgotten, she glanced up to see Emmett coming toward her with two coffees and a white paper bag.

"I found some croissants in the hospital diner," he said. "You need breakfast."

"I need answers," she replied, realizing they'd never had dinner last night. "You eat that."

"I had some food already. And I called and checked on your sisters."

"Are they okay?"

"Your aunt said they're sleeping. They won't go into work at the café today."

Belle let out a sigh of relief. "This has to end. After I talk to Joaquin, I'm going after Lance Johnson and Percy Carolo. I'm going to put them both in a prison cell."

"I can't blame you, but keep calm and let me help," Emmett said. "I've already asked around. There's a traffic camera near the park that could show us if Johnson and Carolo were there."

"That's good," she said, still out for blood. "But I know they were there. I feel it in my gut."

Her parents came back into the waiting area, both looking aged and exhausted.

"He won't tell us anything," Papá said, his gaze close to accusing but he quickly went blank on that. "Maybe he'll talk to you."

Belle stood, every muscle in her body protesting and her heart filled with guilt that she'd let this go so far. "I'll try to get him to tell me what happened." She handed Emmett the coffee she'd barely touched. "I'll see you when I come out."

Emmett touched a hand to her arm. "I'll be here unless I hear something about Randall."

She found Joaquin staring up at the ceiling tiles, a single tear moving down his right cheek.

"How are you?" she asked as she pushed at his thick black hair.

He tugged away. "How do you think?"

"I think you're blessed to be alive," she admitted, hoping bluntness would make him open up to her. "You suffered a near-concussion and you have a cracked rib. Which is probably going to cause you quite a bit of pain for a few weeks."

"The doctor gave me a report, Belle."

"Okay then, this means you can't go running all over town with your former friends, got it?"

"I don't have any friends."

That confession surprised her. "You can have good friends if you're careful."

He didn't respond to that.

"Joaquin, you have to talk to me. I had to report this so we need a statement and—this is very important—you need to tell me the truth."

Her brother's frown crashed against his skin. "I don't want to talk about anything."

Belle shook her head and tugged at her hair. "You have to be honest with me. It's the only way I can help you. Were you with Percy and another man today?"

His dark eyes widened, first in surprise and then in panic. "Who told you that?"

"I'm a cop, little brother. I ask around. People talk, see things. Lance Johnson has made it clear he wants me dead and he's using you to terrorize our family and me. Is that what you want?"

Her brother didn't need to know that she hadn't verified any of this yet. But she needed him to tell her how he'd become involved with these ruthless people.

"No."

The one word came out like a whispered wail.

"Then you'd better start at the beginning and don't leave anything out."

Joaquin swallowed, his fingers clutching the blankets. "Percy found me in the park. Told me he missed seeing the family. Missed you. Asked a lot of questions about you."

Belle managed to keep a blank face even while her jaw muscles tightened. "What did you tell him?"

"That you were still a K-9 cop and you still had an apartment at our house. Stuff like that."

"How did Lance Johnson get involved?"

Joaquin stared at the ceiling again. "Percy came back around and he was with him. A friend, Percy said." He looked into Belle's eyes. "I didn't know, Belle. I didn't get it."

"Get what?" she asked, her heart bumping, her nerves sizzling.

"They told me Emmett wasn't good for you. Stuff about how he was investigating our family and that he was using you. Told me they'd pay me to make him go away."

Go away? They wanted to harm Emmett to get to her?

"What happened, Joaquin?"

"They gave me a hundred-dollar bill to…to scare him and you."

"Scare us? How?"

"The roof, Belle. The chunk of concrete."

Belle stood up and put a hand to her mouth. "You did that? You went onto the roof and threw that broken concrete down at us?"

He nodded, his face contorted with shame and rage. "I wasn't going to hurt either of you, really. I waited until he moved before I dropped it. I just wanted the money."

Belle gulped in air. "You don't worry. I'm going to make sure those two pay much more than a hundred dollars. You could have killed Emmett, Joaquin. You have to know they were lying to you."

"I know that now," he said, his voice rising. "When they came to me again and wanted me to—"

"To what?" she asked, standing at the foot of the bed, her knuckles turning white from gripping the steel frame.

"They wanted me to poison Justice," he blurted out, tears misting over in his eyes. "I couldn't do it. I refused to do it."

White spots of anger dotted Belle's eyes. "So they beat you?"

He nodded. "I got away and hid in the shed."

Belle came around the bed and tugged her brother into her arms. "I'm going to take care of this, understand?"

Joaquin bobbed his head. "I'm sorry."

"I know you are," she whispered. "Now you've learned a valuable lesson. You use this lesson to change your life, okay? To do better, to do good things."

Joaquin looked up at her. "You're not going to arrest me?"

"No, not this time."

Then she let him go and stood. "But I am going after the men who did this to us. You can count on that."

When Belle came out of Joaquin's room, Emmett was gone.

"He got a call. Something about work," her mother said. "Tell me about my son."

Belle pulled her mother close. "He's going to be okay." She explained what had transpired between her brother and her ex. "He told me everything and…I think you'll see a change in him, Mamá. Right now, I have to go."

"Belle, you realize these men have come after our family," her father said. "I'm proud of you for being honest with us and I know you're trained to do this work, but if you don't handle this, I'll find a way."

"No, you will not," her mother said, taking her father's hand. "Enough. Let our daughter bring these two evil men to justice. She's been trained to do that."

Belle appreciated her mother's pride. "She's right, Papá. Stay here and be kind to him. He's afraid and ashamed."

"You check in with us," her mother said.

"I will. I have to pick up Justice and get to work but I'll make sure an officer stays here with you until I can return. Hopefully, this will be over soon."

* * *

Emmett approached the greasy-spoon diner on foot, taking his time to notice the exits and the area around this desolate part of Bay Ridge. One of his informants had seen Randall here again. Emmett had had no choice but to leave the hospital and get here as quickly as possible. He hoped Belle would understand.

He'd called Gavin right away for backup so someone could guard her brother in case she had to leave, too. But Gavin told him Belle had already called in for an officer at the hospital.

"Did she say why?"

"No," Gavin had replied. "Said she'd explain later. Sounded urgent but I think she got a lead. Don't worry. I sent backup to find her."

Now Emmett's thoughts moved from finding Randall to worrying about Belle. He had to remind himself Belle had been doing okay up until now and she'd probably go in with guns blazing to take out the criminals who'd beat up her brother.

If she'd managed to get the truth out of the boy.

Now, he eased his way around the diner's storefront with the appropriate name of Last Stop Hop since it was situated underneath several overpasses. He spotted an NYPD patrol car across the street.

The sound of traffic constantly buzzing against the steel girders and beams overhead blurred with the street noise of people shouting and laughing, moving, always moving. Finding a spot where he had a clear view inside the dingy windows, he searched the sparse mid-morning crowds.

And spotted his cousin Randall sitting at a small table toward the back. Randall wore a Mets cap pulled low over his brow but Emmett knew it was him from his jawline and brawny shoulders. He turned toward the patrol car and nodded to let them know he'd located Randall, then pivoted around.

Before he could make a move, Randall glanced up and saw him, their eyes meeting. Emmett waved and prayed Randall wouldn't bolt out the exit on the other side of the building.

Instead, Randall surprised him by waving and motioning to him.

Emmett entered the diner and took in the few patrons—an older couple arguing about pancakes and traffic. A young mom trying to deal with a crying baby and an older toddler. A bleary-eyed couple in party clothes who looked like they'd been out all night.

The smell of burning coffee and fried bacon assaulted Emmett's senses followed by a musty smell of old, overused furniture and an even older greasy kitchen.

And then there was Randall. He stood when Emmett approached and reached out a calloused hand but he was as jumpy as the grease hitting the hot griddle behind the long counter. "Well, as I live and breathe, Emmett Gage. I haven't seen you in I don't know how long."

"Long time," Emmett said, shaking Randall's hand and noting the tremor that shook it. "How've you been?"

"I've been better," Randall admitted, motioning for Emmett to join him, his eyes darting to the door and all around. "Just having a cup of this mud they call coffee."

The waitress came over, her expression curling in a sneer that pretended to be a smile. "What can I get you?"

"Coffee's fine," Emmett said, glad they served it in real cups. Because he planned to nab Randall's cup somehow.

The weary woman shifted away. Emmett looked over at his distant cousin. "Do you still live around here?"

"Nah, I come and go," Randall allowed, his fingers tapping a nervous jig on the battered tabletop. "Just passing through."

"Where have you been?"

His cousin grew wary, his eyes filling with a dark dread, his hands shaking. He took a sip of coffee and spilled a couple of drops. Randall took the dingy white cloth napkin by his plate and rubbed it over his mouth, then wiped up the spills.

Emmett would bag that, too.

"I've been moving around. Hard to find work anymore at my age but I get by."

But it seemed Randall wanted to hear about Emmett. "What are you doing here, anyway, cuz? How's the family?"

"My parents are both dead now," Emmett said. "I live in Dumbo with two roommates." He explained about his work.

Randall's jitters increased, panic racing across his expression faster than the constant trains at the nearby 59th Street Station jarring the earth as they hummed by.

"Yeah, well, law enforcement runs on your side of the family," Randall said on a bitter note. "Never caught on with my old man. Nor me."

"So you're working still?" Emmett asked, laughing.

Randall bobbed his head, his grin showing two missing teeth, his cough ragged and rough-cut. "I got a friend up in the Catskills. Gives me work here and there in construction and such. He sends me to Brooklyn sometimes to do odd jobs here, too."

They sat silent for a minute while a newsbreak came on the television blaring from a wall-mounted television.

Out of the blue, a report about the Emery murders came on. The pretty newswoman told the tale in a crisp, practiced voice.

"No new leads on the bizarre murder case that rocked Brooklyn a few months ago, but the latest report from the NYPD is that they are getting closer to finding out if the same killer is back in town. Deemed the Emery murders, this heinous crime involved a couple murdered in their home. But the killer left their small child unharmed, even giving the three-year-old girl a stuffed animal."

She went on to talk about the similarities between this case and the cold case from twenty years ago—the McGregors and the little girl the killer had also left behind with a stuffed animal—Penelope McGregor. "The NYPD is currently following a lead on a DNA sample and will check out any and all leads on this case."

Emmett listened and then turned back to Randall, hoping his cousin would say something. But Randall's only response was a telling one.

"I gotta go, man." He got up so quickly the table shifted and people stared. Pushing past Emmett, he said, "I need to get back to work, you know. Good seeing you, Emmett."

"Randall," Emmett said, grabbing his arm. "Wait. You can talk to me. I can help you. If you need anything—"

"I don't need your charity or your pity." Randall yanked away, his congenial mood changing as swiftly as the rainy weather left over from last night. "I need to get outta here."

Emmett tried to block the door, his hand inching toward his weapon. "Randall, I need to talk to you."

Randall pulled a gun from underneath his baggy shirt and waved it in the air. "Nah, I know how this works. They sent you to bring me in."

Emmett held his hands up to calm Randall. "It'll be better if you just go with me to answer some questions."

"I don't think so," Randall said, his hands shaking, his weapon wobbling. Then he turned the gun on the mother and her two suddenly quiet children. A collective gasp went out over the diner. "Let me go, Emmett. I don't want to hurt no one."

Emmett held up his hands again, not about to pull out his own weapon now. "I don't want you to hurt anyone, Randall. But I believe you're in trouble."

"Trouble's been shadowing me all my life," Randall retorted as he backed toward the door, waving the gun at anyone who moved. "You just pretend you never saw me. That's the best thing you can do for me now."

Emmett stood still, keeping watch on all the people who could be in the line of fire. "Randall—"

Randall waved the gun again. "I said, stay back!" Then he gave Emmett a hard glare. "And call off whoever's out there waiting for me. Or I'll have to shoot someone."

Everyone in the café ducked and crouched, afraid for their lives. Emmett tried to see past his cousin to warn the other officers. "Take me, Randall."

His cousin backed out the door, his gun pointing from target to target inside the diner before he held the gun on Emmett. "Let's go."

Emmett went in front of Randall. Randall shoved Emmett with his gun. "Sorry, man. I can't let you take me in." Then he jabbed the butt of his gun against Emmett's head and shoved him against the pavement before he took off on a run, shooting toward Emmett. "Stay away."

Emmett tried to stand but dizziness overtook him. He tried again, pressing his hand against a lamp post. Then he opened the door to the diner.

"Don't clean this table," Emmett called to the wide-eyed waitress as he pulled his gun and spun around after Randall. "I'm coming back."

He spotted Randall heading west and called again, this time with more anger than compassion, his head throbbing with pain. "Randall, stop."

Two officers ran toward them. One shouted, "NYPD. Drop your weapon."

Randall stopped and shot into the air near Emmett and took off around the corner. Then he turned and fired again.

Emmett dived down, frustration heating his gut, dizziness overcoming him. Then he called to the officer. "Go after him."

Dragging himself inside the diner, he held his badge up. "No one leave. The NYPD will need to question you." Then he stood and grabbed the table where he'd been sitting with Randall. "Bring me a plastic bag."

The waitress gave him an evil eye but did his bidding, her scowl now full of fright.

Emmett took a clean napkin and quickly poured what was left of Randall's coffee into the other cup, then bagged the empty cup and the napkin Randall had used.

"Hey, where you taking that mug and napkin?" the waitress asked, her hands on her hip, her tone bullish.

"To the police," Emmett said, deciding that should be explanation enough since he'd flashed his badge and he was bleeding from his temple. He dropped a twenty on the table to take the edge off.

The woman shrugged and grabbed the money, her attitude already rearranging itself.

Emmett pushed away the help the manager offered, took the bagged items and hurried to search the weed-infested empty lot next to the diner. Then he scanned the streets and sidewalks. When he saw one of the officers heading back, shaking his head, dread froze him on the spot. His cousin had disappeared right out from under him. Should he have injured Randall so he could bring him in?

The Brooklyn K-9 Unit might believe he'd let his cousin go. But he had made contact, and from the way Randall had acted, Emmett's gut told him his cousin was the killer of the McGregors.

Gage DNA matched what they'd found on that old watchband and Randall's actions today sealed the deal.

"Sorry, Marshal Gage," the officer said. "He slipped over a fence and then we lost him."

Emmett gave a report to the young man, refused to see a doctor for his busted head and then hurried to his truck. His dad had tried to help Randall and so had he. But he had to remind himself that sometimes a person went beyond wanting to be helped.

And that made his job too tough to handle at times. This would be one of the worst of those times.

SIXTEEN

Emmett sat inside Gavin's office, exhausted and weary, his mood as grim as the rain clouds outside.

Gavin came back in and sank down in his squeaky office chair. "All the witnesses panned out—said the man you were with pulled out a handgun and held it on a woman and two children, then waved it around, threatening everyone in the diner. The waitress said you saved them all by letting him take you out the door with him. The patrol officers saw it all through the window and watched him hit you on the head and run. They tried to capture him—one going one direction and the other following him. He gave them the slip, too, so don't be so hard on yourself."

Emmett shook his head and touched a hand to the bandage he'd found in his first aid kit. "Well, at least I won over the waitress." Then he stared out the window. "I could have shot him."

"You could have," Gavin replied, his tone blank. "But you might have shot him in the back and killed him."

"You know my aim would have been spot on."

"I assume that," Gavin said. "You could have injured him enough to bring him down. But you had others to consider."

Emmett studied Gavin's wall of photos, taking in his wife, Brianne, and their K-9 partners, Tommy and Stella. Other photos of the team showed honors and awards and more wedding moments.

"I hesitated," Emmett admitted. "I wanted to gather evidence and bring him in, not shoot my own kin."

Gavin rubbed his face and studied the papers on his desk before leveling Emmett with a hard glare. "You assured us you'd do your best. I think I should send someone from my unit next time we get a tip on Randall. You're too close to this case. Maybe you need to back off."

A knock at the door brought Belle inside, Justice with her. "Sir, I heard the report."

She spotted Emmett sitting there, his hands cupped, his bandaged head down. "Emmett, are you all right?"

Emmett held up a hand. "I'm fine. Just a scratch."

Gavin came around and shut the door. "We were just discussing what happened."

"I heard you kept Randall from shooting up a whole diner," Belle replied, her tone full of fire as she glanced at Emmett.

"That's true," Gavin said. "He took control of a bad situation, but Gage still got away."

"I can speak for myself," Emmett said, sitting up in his chair. "I bagged his cup and napkin. Your lab is analyzing them and we should know soon if the sample on the watchband found at the McGregor murder site is a true match for his DNA."

Belle sat down in the chair beside Emmett. "I should have been with you. Together and with Justice, we could have caught him."

"I almost had him," Emmett said, "but I had to protect those people in the diner." He held his hands together.

"I had a clear shot when he fired at me and the other officers, but this injury made me question my judgment."

Belle glanced over at Gavin. "So what now, sir?"

"Well, we've put out a BOLO on Randall Gage and we'll keep turning over rocks and searching the streets. But I'm suggesting Marshal Gage steps back to let us handle this."

Emmett stood. "I agree. I messed up. I had one chance and I blew it. Maybe I am too close to this."

His eyes held Belle's. He'd become too close to her, too. He needed to take some time and space and get his head together.

Belle's gaze moved from him to Gavin. "Sir?"

"It's for the best, Belle," Gavin replied. "Whatever you two do on your own time is your business."

Emmett got up. "I'll talk to you later, Belle."

Then he turned and stalked out of the Brooklyn K-9 headquarters, his mind in turmoil, but with a new determination to go back to the work he knew best—tracking wanted criminals.

And he'd start by trying to find his cousin, in his own way.

Belle sat out in the backyard at the family compound, watching Justice sniffing around the yard. She'd sent her parents, sisters and Joaquin, newly released from the hospital, to stay with Uncle Rico until the threat to all of them was over.

"Why aren't you coming with us?" Joaquin had asked when she called to check on him right before his release, his attitude now demure and subdued.

"I won't put any of you in danger again," Belle told

him. "I'm trained to handle these types of situations and Justice will alert me if anyone breaches our property."

Joaquin had nodded. "Uncle Rico said he has people watching out for you, too."

"Oh, yeah, is that right?" Belle's Uncle Rico carried a lot of weight in this neighborhood but in a good way. People respected him and, yes, everyone watched out for each other, per his encouragement. "Tell Uncle Rico I love him," she'd said before ending the call.

Now she sat there thinking that this plan just might work. She'd gotten her family out of the way. Emmett was off trying to find Randall, she knew without him telling her so. She'd seen it in his eyes when he'd left Gavin's office.

She was alone just as she'd been in the park that late afternoon. But this time, she was ready.

"Come and get me," she said into the night. "Because I'm waiting."

These two wanted to slither around like snakes and she was ready to catch one or both of them.

The night cooled down very little but at least a soft breeze kissed at her warm skin. Belle lifted her hair off her neck and took a sip of lemonade. Justice came back and hunkered down beside her. Normally, this was their favorite time of day.

They'd come out for Justice to take a break and then he'd roam for a while before they headed back inside. Now, her little yard took on a sinister feel—shadows sparing with each other, trees shifting as branches scratched and moaned. Voices out on the street around front.

Her phone buzzed, jarring Belle out of her watchful visual.

"Belle Montero."

"Hey."

Emmett. "Hey, yourself. How are you?"

"I've been better," he said. "I told myself to stay away, but I kind of miss you."

"I miss you, too," she admitted. "And I told myself the same thing, but I hope you know you don't have to drop out of my life just because Gavin told you to stay off the case. I know there are boundaries but…we can be friends."

"I'm not dropping out of your life, and I'm certainly not letting this case go. I want to bring in Randall as much as anyone does so I'm casing the areas where he's been seen." He hesitated and then said, "And I'd like to come by and see you. I can still watch out for Johnson and Carolo, too. I have their stats and photos on hand, so I'll know them when I see them."

"Emmett, remember how you warned me to be careful?"

"Yes."

"You do the same."

"I will. What are you doing?"

"I'm sitting on my tiny porch with Justice, enjoying the quiet."

"How is Joaquin?"

"He's fine. He's with my family at my uncle's house about three blocks over. I sent them there for the weekend and I've got a patrol car monitoring them."

"Belle, are you alone?"

"Yes. Is that a hint that you should come over?"

"Do you want me to come over?"

Belle thought about that. She really liked this man. Should she say yes when she'd put herself out here, hoping to lure her attacker?

Could it hurt to have someone watching her back? Or should she give herself and Emmett some time to think this through?

Her stomach tingled with awareness, and then her instincts kicked in. "I'll be okay, Emmett. You don't need to come."

"No, you shouldn't do this alone. I told you I wasn't going anywhere."

"You also told me you can't commit to me," she reminded him.

"That's not exactly what I said, and you know it."

"I heard it, though. You're warning me to stay at a distance and now you're off the case. I have to go."

She ended the call and looked over at Justice. Then she sighed. "I shouldn't have pushed him away, because I think he needs us, boy. We just have to show him that, right?"

She put down her phone, thinking she'd told him the same thing—that she wasn't ready for a new relationship. Even with Emmett, she couldn't break that rule. He might think he could, but she'd believed in Percy's promises and he'd almost destroyed her.

Even with a good man like Emmett, she wasn't ready to risk it again.

So she sat in the dark and wished things could have worked out for them and she also accepted that they might not be able to stay friendly, after all.

A few minutes later Justice stood, startling her. Then her partner growled low and lifted his head toward the alley. Belle shot up out of her chair and scanned the yard. The streetlight behind the fenced wall shimmered an eerie yellow glow. She stilled and listened. When she heard a rustling and what sounded like the gate shifting, she knew someone was behind that fence.

"Seek," she whispered to Justice.

Justice took off toward the fence, barking and snarling.

"That didn't take long," Belle said.

She had her gun ready as she slinked along the fence line and listened, her breath held, her lungs tightening. The fence butted up to the building on each side but there was a gate on the side of the building by her porch. A locked gate.

Justice lifted and scratched at the other gate across the small yard. A gunshot roared through the night and then the gate popped open.

Justice leaped toward whoever had entered. Belle called out, "Attack! Bite!"

Justice followed her command but in the muted light, Belle saw the man. He was dressed in a protective suit.

The kind the team wore in training sessions.

Justice held on, but there was no way he'd get a firm grip on the intruder.

Then she heard another noise.

Someone was trying to scale the fence nearest to the porch.

They were both coming after her.

Emmett had finally secured a parking spot on the street when he heard a shot ring out. Taking out his weapon, he jumped out of his truck and bounded up the porch stoop. "Belle?"

Justice's snarls echoed out over the night. Emmett hurried around the house.

No gate on the right side.

He ran to the left and saw a dark figure running away.

"US Marshal. Stop!"

The man darted over a small chain-link fence into the next yard over and kept running.

Emmett heard Belle's voice. "Justice, halt. Release."

Emmett looked around, trying to figure out how to scale the high wooden fence and then he saw the gate and tried to open it. Still locked. He was halfway up, grunting and trying to find a toehold to jump the fence when he heard Belle again.

"NYPD. Stop," Belle shouted.

Then a gunshot and Justice barking again, angry, snarling barks. The gate at the back of the property slammed shut with a whack.

"Belle?" Emmett called out, his heart dropping, his mind swirling with the worst-case scenario. "Belle?"

The front door swung open with a clatter. "Emmett?"

He dropped away from the fence and rushed around the corner of the yard. Belle stood on the porch, the door open behind her.

Emmett leaped onto the stoop and gathered her close. "Are you all right?"

"Yes. He ran away when he heard you."

"Did Justice injure him?"

"Tried," she said, her breath coming in gulps. "He was wearing protective gear. The other one was trying to come over the front fence."

"I heard a shot."

"I got one in to bring him down. Think I hit his leg but with that gear on, who knows if it went through."

Emmett held her tight while lights came on and people came out of their houses. The whole street went quiet and the night seemed to stand still.

"What are you doing here?" she asked against his shoulder.

"I ignored you telling me to stay away," he said. "Did you honestly think I'd let you do this alone?"

"You got here so quick."

"I'd been circling the block for an hour. I called you from my truck."

"Stubborn."

"Let's get inside," he said, only now catching his breath.

"I have to get Justice in. He's guarding the backyard and people are on the way."

"Okay." He followed her into her apartment but then turned to check the hallway doors. She'd locked all of them, including the one she'd just come back through.

Soon, she had Justice inside and drinking water. Then she turned to Emmett. "I almost had him. I called off Justice and rushed at the man, but he shot and then I shot back. He turned and whirled out the gate, shooting one more time."

She shook her head. "But he screamed at me and told me I'd cost him the woman he loved when I put him in jail. Said he'd get me one way or another. I'm guessing Lance's girlfriend finally left him and now he's blaming me. I think he started watching my routine the minute he got out of jail."

Emmett checked her over and pulled his hand across his moist forehead. "I almost had a heart attack trying to get over that fence. I heard Justice barking and snarling."

"The fence is built to protect and to last," she said, taking him into her arms again. "We rarely unlock either the front or back gates."

Emmett looked down at her and pushed her hair out of

her eyes so he could check to see if she was hurt. Then he leaned down and kissed her, savoring the warmth of her lips and the soft sigh that pushed through her body.

Belle held on to him and then pulled back. "This isn't how I usually do things."

"What do you mean?"

"I've never gotten close to a man during two active cases before. I've never actually had two active cases at one time and I've never been threatened in such an aggressive way."

"There's a first time for everything," he whispered against her ear. "I guess you've never kissed a man who's also involved in such cases before, right?"

"Right. And such a determined man at that."

"Let's try it again, then."

He pulled her back into his arms and kissed her completely and thoroughly. "I think my heart is racing more now than it was before."

Belle nodded in agreement. "How do we handle this, Emmett?"

"Do you want to be with me? To know me?" he asked.

"I don't know... There's so much going on. I didn't think I'd get involved with anyone. Not after my ex did a number on me." Looking up at him, she said, "And I'm not so sure about you. You're too good to be true. I'm waiting for when the bad stuff comes."

Emmett wasn't buying her logic. "First of all, your ex is a horrible example of what love really is. He was pretending at wanting to be a policeman, and even now, he's one of those shadow people who hang around bragging but never actually accomplish anything."

"Except trying to get even with me."

"He hasn't succeeded yet," Emmett reminded her. "He's

tried all the ploys and yet, you're still here. Thankfully." Holding her back so he could look into her eyes, he went on, "And second, I'm not perfect. I have doubts and now you know that. I'm a loner and set in my ways. I travel a lot and I never wanted to settle down with anyone."

"I think that's the part I'm having trouble with. How can I trust that you won't resent me and my work one day?"

"I had a plan, a solid commitment to not get involved with you. But here I am, Belle. I'm not like Percy."

"No, you're not," she said, slapping at his arm. "But I have to be absolutely sure."

He was about to kiss her again to reassure her when they heard voices echoing throughout the hallway.

Belle sighed and laid her head against his chest. "That would be my relatives coming to check on me and just in time. I'm sure the neighbors called my dad since he alerted them that no one would be here tonight. News spreads like a flash flood around here."

"You have a lot of people who love you," he said. Then he thought about that. Could he be one of those people?

SEVENTEEN

They were all talking at once.

Emmett tried to absorb Belle's family moving through the house and up and down the stairs while he also worked to keep up with the two members of her unit who'd shown up to search her yard, coming and going while they talked into their radios. He had sensory overload since his parents had been stoic, quiet and stern most of the time. That had taught him to savor quiet and solitary moments. He felt in the way and out of place here amid so much action, but he also knew the procedure. Emmett had to get back out there, and he might have to do it on his own.

If he could find a way through this crowd.

"You're going to get yourself killed," Belle's mother kept saying, her hands waving more and more with each repetition. "This is too much, Belle." Then she lapsed into Spanish, explaining why Belle needed to get married and settle down.

Emmett didn't think that would happen anytime soon. She would have stopped him from kissing her back there even if her folks hadn't shown up. And all because he'd told her the truth—falling for a woman as bold and brave as her could be the most dangerous thing he'd ever done.

Belle looked as if she wanted to scream.

"Belle, we need you outside," K-9 Detective Tyler Walker, who'd brought his golden retriever, Dusty, to help track the intruders, called out. Her friend Noelle had also arrived on the scene with her K-9, Liberty, but Gavin assigned her to crowd control in the house. Others were canvassing the yard and streets and knocking on doors to see if anyone had seen two suspicious men lurching about.

Looking relieved, Belle started toward the back door.

"Belle, why did you stay here like some lamb to be sacrificed?" her father asked, his salt-and-pepper hair standing straight up in a jagged ruffle on his head.

Her twin sisters sat on the stairs, leaning on each other, tired and worried. Every now and then, they'd both shot a look at Emmett, their dark eyes pleading for answers.

"I'm fine," Belle said to her parents. "I have to get to work."

"Work. Work to do. That is her way." Mrs. Montera threw up her hands one last time and stalked toward the stairs. "I'll go up and make everyone something to eat."

Belle kissed her father and then turned to head back out.

Emmett stood staring after Belle, wishing they hadn't been interrupted earlier. But neither of them was ready to admit anything. Plus, they had to gather evidence and track footprints and try to find these aggressors.

He knew that better than anyone. So he turned and started out the back door, determined to work his own grid like he'd done a hundred times with criminals.

"Hey." A voice called out behind him. Emmett turned to find Joaquin standing in the hallway, his hands in the pockets of his jeans.

"What's wrong?" Emmett asked, wondering if the boy was still keeping secrets. He looked dejected and…guilty.

"I might know something," Joaquin said, lowering his head.

"Something like what?" Emmett asked.

"I heard them talking once, arguing, when they were trying to beat me to a pulp."

Emmett saw the black eye and cuts still healing on the boy's face. "What did you hear?"

"Percy said something about a house over near the park. I think it's abandoned but he's been sneaking Lance Johnson in and out. He said something about getting the stuff they needed and hiding it there." Brushing at his hair, Joaquin finally looked up at Emmett. "They planned to dump me there, you know, after they'd killed me."

Emmett heard the fear in the boy's words. "Have you told anyone else this?"

"I didn't remember at first. Things keep coming to me now, though. I know the address."

After he memorized the address Joaquin gave him, Emmett stepped closer and moved the teenager out onto the porch. "Listen, I know you're scared but you can't live in fear. You have to tell the truth, or this could get worse."

"How can I do that now?" Joaquin said. "I almost died over trying to make easy money."

"You learned a hard lesson," Emmett said. "Take that and make something out of it. Walk inside the light—no more trying to make easy money."

"What can I do?"

"You keep remembering things that might help us and we'll keep fighting them. They'll mess up sooner or later and we'll end this."

Joaquin's shoulders lifted. "I'll do my best. I love my sister."

"I know you do. You just watch your back," Emmett

told him. Then he handed Joaquin his card. "And you call this number if you ever need me, understand?"

The boy nodded and put the card in his pocket.

"Joaquin?" His sister Anita's voice lifted out over the night.

"Coming." He gave Emmett a shy glance and hurried inside.

Emmett glanced around and remembered the front fence where one of the intruders had been trying to break in. He headed over to examine it, using his flashlight to see what he could find.

Footprints on the ground all around the gate, but then he'd stepped in this same spot so his would be there, too. Holding the light up to the worn wood, he noticed a strip of fabric dangling from a crooked nail.

Emmett held the light close and noticed the print on the material. Tugging in his pocket for some latex gloves, he put his light down long enough to put them on. Then he gently lifted the torn material off the fence.

Part of an emblem or patch clung to the torn material. A uniform maybe. Then a memory came to him. A uniform from a certain storage unit located across town? He squinted in the sharply focused light. It just might be a match.

He'd give this to the crime scene techs. Maybe they could find some DNA on this and match it to Percy Carolo.

That would be another win for the growing pile of possible evidence linking Belle's ex to her attacker.

The fence had held and thankfully, when he'd shown up, they'd both run away like the cowards they were. They thought they could take Belle, but she'd proven them wrong.

That thought scared him enough to make him see that

he did care about her and with more than just a feeling of friendship. That also meant he had to keep her safe, whether she or these intruders liked that.

Belle stood at attention the next morning when Gavin entered his office. Her colleagues and friends Lani Jameson and Jackson Davison stood with her. They'd been called in for an assignment.

Belle liked having Lani and her partner, Snapper, with her, and Jackson worked with Belle in Emergency Services. He looked fresh and clean, his dark hair crisp and his green eyes always flashing in that guarded way she'd come to know. His chocolate Lab, Smokey—one of Stella's famous pups and now trained in cadaver detection—sat on his haunches by Jackson's side.

Were they going to search for bodies?

Lani shot Belle a questioning glance while Gavin came around his desk, her blue eyes bright with questions.

"Sit," Gavin said as he eased into his chair. Then he looked directly at Belle. "I called you three in this morning because we've gained new evidence regarding the roving harassment team of Johnson and Carolo."

Belle leaned in. "Did the techs find something last night, sir?"

"Your friend the marshal found something," Gavin said, his tone firm while his eyes softened. "He gave a scrap of material to one of the crime scene techs. Turns out it's from a uniform. That, added to your brother's testimony and all the information you've gathered, should be enough for a warrant to enter Percy Carolo's home."

Belle took in his words and wondered why Emmett hadn't come to her about this. But then, he'd gone off on his own last night and she'd been busy with the techs and keeping her family calm. Had her family drama scared him away?

Or had their kisses scared him in the same way they'd scared her?

"What did the material show?" she managed to ask.

"A lot, all things considered. It's from a uniform that Percy Carolo obviously still had on. From the City Wide Storage unit."

"Bingo," Jackson said. "That's the one right, Belle? Where you and the marshal were ambushed?"

"Yes." She couldn't believe Percy would go to such lengths to get even with her. "So Johnson had on the protective suit and Percy planned to come through the front and probably take me down while Justice was distracted."

"That's what we believe," Gavin said. "After your brother gave him a location near the park he'd heard the two men talking about, Emmett came up with his own plan of attack. He wants to bring these men in so he can get back to finding his cousin."

"Emmett?" Belle shook her head. No way Emmett would take over this case. He had no right. "This is my case, sir. I can handle this. He shouldn't have come to you since he's off the cold case, per your request."

"He wants you to be safe," Gavin said, keeping his voice neutral but controlled. "He gave me the evidence and suggested a plan to put a surveillance team on the abandoned house they've been using. The man does know how to capture criminals, Belle. I never doubted he'd keep searching for his cousin, but on his own time."

Belle tried to digest this, her heart screaming right along with the thoughts shouting inside her head. Emmett wanted this over so he could get back to finding his cousin? But he wanted her safe. Did he care about her?

Their kisses indicated he did, but was he just doing his duty since he'd been involved from the beginning? He was the kind of man who'd do the right thing, even when he wanted to be elsewhere.

"He can't keep me out of this," she finally said. "Whatever he's planned without me, I want in."

Gavin let out a sigh and lifted his eyebrows. "That's why you're here, Officer."

Belle settled back. "So what's the plan?"

Gavin glanced up and nodded. "I'll let him tell you himself. Come in, Marshal Gage."

Belle whirled to find Emmett standing there. She'd get to him later. "Why don't you go ahead, sir," she said to the chief.

Emmett stepped farther into the room and spoke instead. "After I checked out the house and found it empty, the plan was to have Lani and Jackson patrol the park and the house where these two miscreants hang out, hoping to nab them. But—"

"But I'm the one who needs to do that, sir," Belle said, turning from Gavin to glare at Emmett. "And I don't care what Marshal Gage thinks about that. I want in on this. Lance Johnson came after *me* and then he hooked up with the worst person possible—a man who's had it in for me since I walked out of his life a few years ago. He finally found a way to get back at me."

Then she stood and dared anyone to argue with her. "But I'm going to take them both down and I hope you'll allow me to do that." Her gaze centering on Emmett, she added, "To do *my* job."

Gavin stood and they all followed suit. "You heard my officer, Marshal Gage. She's in. No discussion. I'd like to believe I'm still in charge of this unit, after all."

Emmett looked at Belle and then nodded at Gavin. "Sorry I overstepped. Of course, Officer Montera would want in on this. After all, she's the target."

He said that in a way that expressed concern and acceptance. He wanted to protect her, but Belle had to do this herself. Had he planned this whole thing so he could be in on capturing these men with her? To show her how much he cared? Or to make a point that he knew better than her?

She wanted to believe he cared and she also wanted to believe he understood she was perfectly capable of handling this. Right now, her brain couldn't deal with all the emotions roiling over in her stomach. She had an assignment. She would follow through.

"Yes, I'm the target," Belle said, whirling away from her coworkers to confront Emmett. "And I'm going to be the bait this time."

She saw the flare of concern in his beautiful silvery-blue eyes, but she ignored it. He wanted to protect her, and she wanted to do the same for him. How could they ever compromise and have a relationship when they lived with danger each and every day? Maybe this was more proof that they didn't belong together.

Emmett gave her a resigned appraisal. "Then let's come up with a plan." He briefed them on the location of the house and went over the plans for the park.

Belle felt both relief and dread wash over her. This had to end so her family would feel safe again. And so she could finally explore her conflicting feelings for Marshal Emmett Gage.

EIGHTEEN

"Remember, you're patrolling the park, nothing more," Jackson reminded Belle later that day. "We've put out the word that we're cracking down on illegal activities in this particular park and we have people watching the abandoned house. A kid was attacked here, and the NYPD wants to put an end to that kind of violence."

Her brother—the kid who was attacked. But they hadn't put out his name, thankfully.

"Got it," Belle said as they pulled up and parked off-site, both their partners waiting in the back of the SUV. "You'll patrol with me, but I'll be on the other side of the block where I can see you at all times." Belle took a deep, calming breath.

"Yes, and Emmett and Lani will be dressed in plain clothes, a couple out walking their dog."

"Except their dog is Snapper, and the highly trained German shepherd is good at his job," Belle added with a streak of vengeance.

"It's going to be over soon, Belle," Jackson said. "We'll all make sure of that."

Her phone buzzed. *Emmett.*

"Belle Montera," she said in her most professional voice.

"I know you're mad at me but—"

"That is correct, and I can't talk right now."

"Belle, I want you safe."

"Because you want to move on to the bigger concern. I get it."

"No, you don't get it, but you will," he said. "When this is over, I'll show you what I mean."

"I'm not planning on that."

"Stay safe, Belle. For me, okay?"

She had to admit the plea in his words got to her.

"I'm going to do my level best."

She ended the call and glanced over at Jackson.

"You okay?" he asked, a slight smile on his face.

"Never better. Let's get this over with."

They got out of the vehicle, and Jackson hit the key fob to let their partners out. This was a sign to both dogs that it was showtime. Smokey danced in excitement and Justice stood staring up at Belle, his dark eyes curious and full of anticipation.

"You two are the best," she said to the smart animals. "We're going to do our jobs, and I want you to stay safe."

Jackson nodded to her. "You do the same, Belle."

They parted and Belle started along with Justice, allowing him a loose leash in case he spotted someone. He'd pick up on the familiar scents of the men who'd tried to break into her family's property and she had to remember Justice was trained to do his work, too. Since he'd been hit with that tranquilizer dart the night she met Emmett, she'd feared for her partner. Thankful that her attacker hadn't killed Justice last night, she prayed for strength and courage.

And protection.

Your unit members are listening in, she reminded herself. *Justice will be safe. I have to trust in God's protection, too.*

She had a whole community praying for her since her mother had a very long prayer chain.

They'd purposely waited until an hour before dusk since that was prime time for park gatherings around here. Belle walked along at a casual pace, glancing here and there to see if she was being followed.

When a group of teenagers appeared near the old basketball court, Belle took notice. Justice sniffed and deemed them not what he was searching for, so she did a crisscross through the park and stopped here and there so the kids would know she was official. They scattered, mumbling to themselves. Belle recognized a couple of boys who hung out with Joaquin now and then.

Thinking her brother had been very brave by telling her the truth and giving Emmett more information, she prayed for him, too. It was tough being a teen in this neighborhood, but she'd survived. She wanted her only brother and the twins to do the same.

After an hour, the sun began descending through the trees to the west. Belle was about to give up.

"I got nothing," she said into her mic, pretending she was talking to Justice.

"We're still here but no word from the house." *Emmett.* He'd been trying to talk to her, but she wasn't in the mood. Belle had watched Emmett and Lani, laughing and talking as they sat on a bench across from where she patrolled, Snapper calm by Lani's side. Then they'd walked around the perimeters of the park and ignored her as she'd done the same. Yet, she felt his eyes on her, knew he was watching through his sunshades. She'd have to forgive him. His intentions were good, after all. And truth be told, she did feel safe with him nearby.

She had to admit, she was falling for the man and she'd fought it every step of the way.

She rounded a corner and came close to where they'd found Joaquin in the old shed. Her heart pumped with fear for her brother as she flashed back to that night. Emmett had been right there with her.

Emmett.

He'd been with her through this whole ordeal and he'd come to her rescue over and over. But she'd acted like an ungrateful brat today.

She couldn't say that with others listening in.

"I'm not giving up," she said to anyone who could hear. "I mean it."

"I'm not, either," Emmett replied.

Had they just made their peace?

Before she could relax on that thought, Justice bristled.

Then a flash exploded, and smoke shot out everywhere. Belle's eyes filled with the thick, cloying gray fog, burning so she couldn't see. Her throat clogged with the stench of chemicals, mainly sulfur. Justice barked and snarled. A smoke bomb!

Jackson called out behind her. "Belle?"

Someone grabbed her and forced the leash out of her hand.

"You're mine now. It's good to have you in my arms again, Belle."

Percy.

Belle tried to squirm away, but he put something over her face and she passed out.

Her last thought was of Justice and Emmett. Her two protectors. Would they be able to save her this time?

* * *

Emmett heard a man's voice over the static of the radio. "Something's wrong." He tore away from Lani and took off toward the smoke rising across the park. He figured it was a smoke bomb before he saw the cylinder-style container lying on the sidewalk.

Lani reported their status and hurried after him, Snapper leading the way.

Jackson sprinted across the park, calling the location as he ran. Smokey barked and hustled along with him. "I was a few yards behind her. He took her."

Emmett stopped where the smoke still hung heavy in the air, the heavy fog settling into his lungs.

"She's gone," he said, glancing around to find Justice's leash lying on the broken sidewalk near the shed where they'd found Joaquin a few days ago. "They took her and Justice."

He couldn't believe he'd let her do this—put herself out there like this—knowing these two men wanted her dead.

He'd never forgive himself if he couldn't find her.

Lani came back from the old storage shed and touched his arm. "Think, Emmett. She's not in the shed but the dogs are restless. Whoever took Belle might still have her nearby."

"You're right," he said. Then he heard a dog barking. "Justice."

They took off past where Jackson still worked the shed, searching inside and all around. "Nothing here to help," he said, following them.

They found Justice hidden behind an old oak with what looked like a fishing net thrown over him. Someone had tied him to the tree. Justice struggled to get loose. Emmett quickly freed the big dog, glad he wasn't harmed.

Lani took over. "Justice, find."

Justice knew what to do. He took off into the bramble and the saplings, his barks loud and anxious.

Emmett and Lani followed while Jackson stayed behind to alert the first responders.

"The house," Emmett said as they sprinted into the weeds and underbrush. "The abandoned house. They must have taken her there." He shouted out the address again.

Someone responded. "We've got movement inside the house."

"Justice must be taking us there," Lani replied, her blond bun bouncing as they jogged.

Thankful for her long legs, Emmett kept up with her while they searched the surrounding houses. But Justice kept trotting, glancing back to make sure they were following.

Emmett prayed the dog had the right scent.

He had to find Belle before it was too late.

Belle woke, disoriented and groggy, sick and nauseated.

Blinking, she looked around the dank, stifling room and wondered where she was. Then it all came back. The park, the smoke bomb, Percy drugging her, knocking her out.

She tried to move and realized her left hand had been cuffed to a flimsy chair back.

Struggling to sit up, Belle tried to get her bearings. She reached for her radio. Gone. Her phone. Also gone. Her weapons had been removed from her uniform.

"Hello?" she called, her pulse drumming heavily against her temple, her breath coming in great huffs while she tried to think, to find a way out.

The windows were covered with tan paper—the kind

used to wrap boxes for mailing. The scents of body odor
and stale food assaulted her, along with the smell of decaying
wood and old leaves and moist dirt. Sweat moved like
a clawing hand down her back and across her shoulders.

"I have to get out of here," she whispered.

"I don't think so."

Lance Johnson walked through some old tattered curtains
from another room. "You're hard to kill, Officer
Montera. But now I have you right where I want you."

"Where's Percy?" she asked, knowing this would not
go well.

"Oh, so you do miss your ex? He told me all about
you two."

Johnson knelt by where she sat on the old mattress. "He
said you like to put strong men in their place. Made him
feel less than with all your bluster and bragging. I know
how that feels since you wrongfully sent me to prison."

"You were guilty," Belle pointed out. "I caught you
beating up your girlfriend."

"My ex-girlfriend now," he said, grabbing Belle by the
arm. "I swore I'd get even with you when she broke up
with me and left the city."

"Well, you've certainly made a mess of that," Belle
retorted, her need to survive overcoming her anxieties.
She knew her team members would show up and she
certainly knew that Emmett would be with them. Justice
would find her.

Her prayers held tight, surrounding her, filling her
head.

We do not live in a spirit of fear.

Johnson shoved her against the back of the chair, causing
her neck to snap and her head to hit hard against the
old wood. "Percy is going to pay me a big amount of

money for helping him to find you. He wants to talk to you, so he'll be here soon."

Bile rose in Belle's throat. Percy would want revenge, too.

"Tell him I'll be waiting," she said, spitting each word out in a rage that left her breathless.

Johnson laughed and whirled to leave.

"Wait," Belle called. "Was that you on the motorcycle?"

"Yes. But it's long gone. Turned into scrap."

"So you used a stolen motorcycle to spy on me and you followed me to the park that day?"

His smug grin showed malice. "Easy to do. Just watch and wait."

"And you waited at the precinct later that night and tried to run me down on that same bike?"

"Maybe."

He didn't lie very well.

"I have to get out of here," he said. "Percy made it clear he wanted me gone before he comes back."

Belle watched him go, then took in her surroundings and went to work on getting herself free. The old high-back chair didn't have the strength to hold her, so she managed to twist around enough to start poking at one of the skinny posts. They'd cuffed her with enough of a chain to give her a little movement, so she used that to her advantage by standing in a stooped position. Each kick and jab seared her cuffed wrist, the digging pain shooting all the way up her neck to make her wince. But she would not die here in this desolate place.

Emmett's heart pounded with all the intensity of bullets hitting concrete. He had to find Belle. The images in his head weren't good ones. He'd dealt with enough deranged, vengeful men to know how things could go. Carolo and Johnson would taunt her and then kill her.

Dear God, help us all now.

They moved through woods and yards and stomped through messy drainage areas, but Justice didn't stop. The big dog seemed honed in on one scent, one thing, one way.

All around, Emmett heard others roaming through the dusk, shadows deepening, voices carrying, people shouting. Neighbors staring at them and calling out. The SWAT unit pulled up around the corner, ready to roll.

He kept going, focusing on the steps, putting the horrible thoughts out of his head. Wishing he'd told Belle how he felt about her, wishing he'd said so many things to so many people.

But he had to find Belle and be honest with her. He wanted to stay around her, spend time with her. Love her.

Yes, he could admit that he'd fallen and hard. Never saw that coming and not so quickly, either. They still had so much between them, but he was willing to wade his way through all of it for her.

Emmett stumbled over a broken crack in the sidewalk.

Then he looked up and found Justice standing alert, his head up, his ears pitched forward, his gaze on the old abandoned house on the corner, back from the street. The address Joaquin had given him.

Emmett held up his hand to those all around. Then he pointed to the dog and the house.

Shouts came over the radio. Locations. Positions. "Move in the SWAT team. Get here ASAP."

Please, get here fast. That thought echoed in Emmett's head as he slowly made his way toward the boarded-up, beaten-down house.

NINETEEN

Belle heard a noise in the other room. Quickly, she positioned herself on the chair, willing her heart to settle. Her bruised wrist throbbed against the cuff.

But she was ready now.

The curtains curled back, crackling with age and mold.

"Well, well, it's been a long time, hasn't it, sweet Belle?"

Percy stood there in jeans and a dark T-shirt, his black eyes burning with hatred and rage, his inky ebony hair long and rakish. "I know you must have missed me a little bit."

"Not all that much," she retorted, so ready to end this even while her heart rate accelerated. "And by the way, chasing me, threatening me and hiring some lowlife to try to kill me didn't make me any fonder of you, Percy."

"I don't know what you're talking about."

"Yes, you do," Belle said as he inched closer, the smell of his cheap aftershave making her gag. "You put the envelope underneath my door, didn't you? Because you kept a copy of the key I gave you, right?"

"Well, I did help you install the security system years ago, and I figured you'd changed the code and the lock. But I sent Johnson to do the job. Slipped right in after your brother opened the front door and jogged right on upstairs without a clue."

"We do have a new key code now," she retorted. "And better security. I'm a different woman. Stronger, more secure, a lot smarter."

"You might think you're smart," he said through a hiss as he yanked her up and shook her shoulders. "But you're the one cuffed to that chair, aren't you?"

Belle waited until he was leaning over her and then she lifted her now uncuffed hand away from the broken chair spindle she'd managed to stick back up against the old backing. "Not anymore, Percy."

Then she grabbed the spindle and hit him hard against the head. She knew she hadn't done too much damage but it was enough get him away so she could squirm up and run. Running as fast as she could, she almost made it to the front door.

Then barking outside and a commotion stopped her. Justice!

Belle screamed out, her hand on the doorknob. If she could open it, Justice would be able to help. Her adrenaline high, she called out in hope. "Justice, Attack."

But Percy tackled her, and her hand slipped away from the locked door.

Emmett heard a faint scream and then watched as Justice leaped into the air and put a bite-hold on the man trying to sneak around the corner of the house.

Lance Johnson cried out in pain, screaming and begging Justice to let him go.

Jackson hurried by, headed toward the dog and the man writhing in pain on the ground. "I got this, Marshal Gage. Go in and find Belle."

Confused, Emmett realized Belle wanted Justice to come into the house. But the K-9 had done his job out here. He'd captured Lance Johnson. So that meant someone else had Belle inside the house.

The grim weight of that hit Emmett in his gut. Percy Carolo would enjoy tormenting Belle, especially if he knew her entire unit was right outside.

Emmett was headed up the cracked steps when he heard a voice through one of the broken window panes where stained paper hung tattered and shredded, leaving partial views into the house. "Don't come any closer or I'll kill her."

Emmett saw the silhouette in the waning shadows. A man holding a woman against his chest, a gun pressed against her rib cage.

Belle.

"What do you want?" Emmett called out, holding a hand behind him to warn the others. "Just tell me."

Percy Carolo chuckled hard and fast. "I want my Belle back."

"I don't want *you*," Belle said to Percy, her eyes on Emmett. She spoke firmly, a cut on her lip, blood seeping down her face. "Percy, you need to let me go or things will only get worse for you."

"Worse?" Percy yanked her closer, one hand pressed across her chest. "How much worse could it get? I hired an inept stooge to help me get to you, and he failed at every attempt. He couldn't even kill you in the park before I met him."

Emmett inched closer, not daring to take his eyes off them. But darkness was settling like a moldy blanket all around this house. He couldn't let this man take Belle away.

Behind him, Lance Johnson cried out. "Carolo made me do all of it. Hired me to harass her and kill the dog, talked her brother into helping. I told him I tried to get rid of her in the park, but he wants her all to himself before he does the job."

"Shut up," Jackson told the bleeding man as he hauled him toward where an ambulance waited. "You can spill your guts in court."

Emmett called out again. "What do you really need right now, Carolo? Time's wasting out here."

"I got what I want."

Emmett gritted his teeth at that comment. But he pulled himself together. "Then I'll stay right here because we have you surrounded, Carolo. And your buddy Lance is squealing like a pig."

Carolo shoved Belle toward the window, then stood behind her, his weapon pointed at her. "I told you, I'll kill her if you do anything more than breathe."

"I'm not doing anything," Emmett said, praying Belle's unit members had things under control. "But I can't speak for the Brooklyn K-9 Unit and the SWAT team moving in now. You see, I'm a US marshal and I'm trained to bring in people who break the law." He paused, let out a sigh. "And we all plan to bring you in for assault and battery on an officer, attempted murder and kidnapping. That's just the first page."

"So you'll bring me in—and you don't care if I shoot her first?" Percy cursed and shouted, "You tell all of them to back off and let me alone. I need to think. I mean it. If anyone comes close to this house, it's over. If I die, so does she."

Emmett held his breath, his mind whirling. He knew

Justice was standing guard behind him. But how did he get the K-9 into the house?

"I'm backing away, Carolo," he called. "But I'll be nearby. Everyone else has moved away."

"Keep them back," Carolo called. "I have to come up with a new plan."

Emmett had to do the same. Come up with a new plan.

How did he save the woman he'd fallen in love with from a madman who only wanted to make her suffer before he killed her?

Belle clung to the sure knowledge that Emmett was on the other side of that door. She'd been so close to escaping when Percy had grabbed her and hauled her back, slapping her hard for daring to try.

Now he held her there by the window as a shield while he watched the night shadows outside, threatening anything that moved. It hurt so much to know people she cared about were close and she couldn't reach them. But she wasn't going to sit here all night with a man who'd gone from bitter to irrational.

Where was Emmett?

"Your new man is out there," Percy said, as if reading her very thoughts. "I don't get you, Belle. I thought we had something special." He rubbed his dark hair and gave her a perplexed stare. "When I saw you with him going through a storage unit, I went berserk all over again. Right there under my nose but as it turned out, a perfect coincidence."

"So you called your new friend and my enemy, Lance Johnson, to help you take out both of us?"

"I knew Johnson would leap on that," Percy said. "But he's an idiot. Can't shoot anything but his own foot." Then he changed, his voice whining and soft. "We could fix all of this if you'll just go away with me."

Belle gave him a look of disbelief. "Percy, you were abusive to me and you hated that I got a promotion. We had nothing special." Then she raised her voice. "I'm not going anywhere with you."

He leaned down and stared in her face, waving his gun in the air where he forced her to sit in a chair centered in the window. He could pace in front of her knowing the sharpshooters wouldn't shoot through her. "You're wrong. We had everything until you left me. Lance told me you did the same thing to him, caused his girl to leave him."

"He beat her. You came close to that with me, remember? Women don't put up with that stuff these days."

"No, no. We just had a little spat. Baby, you know I love you. I'll always love you."

Belle didn't respond to that. The man was seriously deranged. But she did watch his every step and she counted how many steps she'd need to jump through that shattered window and get away. If she just gave him time to move to the other side of the room, she thought she could make it.

It might be her only chance to get out of here alive.

Emmett stood with Jackson and the rest of the team. They planned to charge the house but…they had to find the right time. He'd studied the layout enough to know the bottom floor held a kitchen and large living room, where Percy had taken Belle.

"We can storm in there and hope he doesn't hurt her," Gavin told them earlier. "Or we can wait it out. SWAT is ready to do whatever we need."

"Negotiating won't get us anywhere," Emmett said. "We can't sweat him out, but he might get hungry."

"He might start making demands," Gavin said. "It's been two hours and he hasn't made a move other than pacing in front of that window. But we can't shoot him—too risky with Belle there as his shield."

"He knows I'm not alone," Emmett said, the thought of Belle getting shot making him want to go into action. "He's keeping her alive for some reason. I'd like to believe he has a soft spot in that black heart."

Or the man just wanted to drag out the torment and fear.

Emmett stared toward the house. The yellow glow of a street lamp showed the true hero. Justice sat hunched at the bottom of the steps. The dog refused to leave without his partner.

Emmett looked around at the people who'd gathered here, their emergency lights off and their vehicles out of sight. "There is one other thing that could happen."

"What's that, Marshal?" Lani asked.

"Belle might be waiting for the chance to save herself. And that scares me more than anything else."

Gavin stared back at the house and then glanced back at Emmett. "You're right. She's capable of doing that, but just in case, when she does, we'd better be ready to move in."

Belle had to make her move. They'd been inside the house for three hours now and Percy's agitation was growing by the minute. "I can get us both out of here," she said, trying to stand.

Percy whirled, his gun pointed. "I'm not falling for that trick. You and I both know how this works. If I open that door or make a wrong move, I'm toast. They probably have a sniper on me right now just waiting for the command to take me out."

"I haven't seen a red spot on your forehead yet," Belle said, thinking the same thing. "They don't want to kill you, Percy. They have Johnson. He's going to blame you. But they want you alive to hear your side of things."

Percy pushed at his damp hair, then jabbed a finger in the air. "He started this. I just met him while he was in prison. I worked there briefly as a guard, but man, I hated working at Rikers. They never saw my worth. After Lance got out, we met up again at the gym and then we went to a bar and put two and two together. All he talked about was how he'd make you pay. I wanted in on that."

"I thought you loved me," she said, knowing he never had loved her at all. "But instead, you decided to threaten me and my family and now you want to kill me?"

"I do love you, Belle," Percy said, pushing her back against the wall. "Enough to kill both of us and end it here."

Belle stared at him and, even in the moonlight, saw the hatred in his eyes. "Neither one of us needs to die and…I can help you get away."

Percy's eyes widened. "Do you mean it? Have you had a change of heart?"

Belle thought of Emmett and willed her expression to soften. "Yes, a big one."

"So what's the plan?" Percy asked, his hand touching her hair, his dark eyes burning with a madness she couldn't tolerate. "'Cause if you're playing me, I'll know it."

Belle held back the cringe that rumbled down her spine and gave Percy her best smile. "Just this," she said, rising out of the chair, her hands on his meaty arms guiding him so he had to face away from the street to keep her near. She motioned him toward her, a smile hiding the revulsion coiling through her.

As he moved close, she pressed against the opposite wall behind her in the tiny room. Just as he lowered his head to kiss her, Belle shoved him hard and lifted one of her legs with a high kick to Percy's midsection. He flew back toward the front window where he'd been holding her and dropped his gun. Grabbing the weapon, Belle put it in her belt. Then she hurled herself at Percy and flipped him down onto his back underneath the open window, stomping her boot in his back while she lifted the chair and smashed the remainder of the window into bits. A gaping hole of fresh hot air greeted her. Freedom.

"Justice," she called, her boot still digging into Percy's back while he moaned. "Come. Attack."

Her partner lifted into the air and sailed through the open window to land a foot away from where Percy moaned on the floor.

Justice then added to the moans when he bit into Percy's jeans.

Belle let out a shuddering breath as the house exploded with K-9s and their partners. The dogs surrounded Percy so she called Justice off and then turned as Emmett rushed in the door and parted the crowd. Giving her a quick glance, he kept moving toward the man curled in a ball in the corner.

He lifted Percy Carolo off the floor and snarled at him. "Let me do the honors, please." Then he told Percy he was under arrest for harassing and assaulting an officer, for the attempted murder and kidnapping of said officer, just as he'd stated earlier. Then he read him his rights and cuffed him before shoving him toward Jackson.

"I'll get him out of here," Jackson said, grabbing Carolo by his sweat-soaked collar.

"Belle, you betrayed me again," Carolo shouted. "I will kill Lance Johnson when I find him."

Belle gave him a look of pity but decided he'd find out soon enough how things worked with the law.

Belle stood by the window while the EMT checked her out, her adrenaline sliding away with each breath she took. Lani hugged her and let her be. Jackson nodded to her and did his job. Gavin came in and stood staring at her.

"I'm all right," she kept saying, her eyes always shifting to Emmett.

Emmett moved around the officers filing through the house and hurried to pull her into his arms. He held her there until both of their hearts beat a new rhythm.

Together.

TWENTY

Belle woke up late the next morning, her body sore, her mind at peace. It was over. Lance Johnson would go back to jail for a long time and even if he got out, he wouldn't dare mess with her again.

Percy Carolo would probably meet the same fate since they had enough evidence to put him away for a long, long time. He'd still blame her, but both Emmett and Gavin had explained to him in no uncertain terms that if he ever came near Belle again, he'd regret it in a big way.

Last night, they'd all gone to the precinct to file reports and question both of her attackers. Her ordeal was over but Sarge had announced that someone had tried to run over Liberty, the yellow Lab K-9 with a bounty on her head, last night while several of them were trying to save Belle. Noelle had taken her partner for a walk when it had happened. Now Noelle's street and home would be monitored around the clock. Belle wanted in on that.

She said a prayer for Noelle.

She rolled over and saw Justice lying in his home kennel near her bed. She'd left the kennel door open because he seemed to want to follow her around, still in protection mode.

But she had to wonder about her other protector.

Would he stick around now that the danger was gone? He'd made it clear he wanted to get back out there and find his cousin. But where things stood between them, she couldn't say.

Emmett had brought her home after she'd given her statement and Gavin had ordered her to take the rest of the week off.

Emmett waited while she took a shower. Her mother sent down food but left them alone. Emmett told her to eat.

Then he went upstairs and explained to her parents and siblings about what had happened, assuring them she was okay and they were safe. Uncle Rico could call off his guards.

Emmett came back and held her close for a while, silent and strong and sure. "We can talk later," he told her. "We have a lot to talk about. Right now, you need to rest and sleep."

Belle loved being there in his arms. She did fall asleep on the couch, her head pressed against his chest.

After a while, Emmett lifted her up and tucked her into bed with a kiss. "I'll see you soon, I promise."

Then he kissed her one last time and headed to the door.

Belle could only nod, her emotions and the letdown that always came after a big arrest being twice as difficult this time. She wanted to tell him that she'd thought about him the entire time she'd been held in that house with Percy.

But she couldn't be sure if Emmett wanted the same. He must. He'd stayed there outside the house, watching over her.

He'd come back to her, wouldn't he?

* * *

He had to give her some space. That had been the hardest thing to do. Leaving Belle last night had torn Emmett's heart apart, but he still had some unfinished business out here.

Emmett had work to do, but he wanted to see Belle and make sure she was all right. She was tough but even a tough person could only take so much.

She'd been chased and harassed and shot at over the last couple of weeks—and almost killed. How did a person put that behind and get on with life?

And how did they stop these careening emotions and feelings that had exploded between them in the heat of the chase?

Could they sustain those feelings now that things had settled back down? He wanted that, wanted to be with Belle. But he had to find Randall first.

After checking in at his office and getting ribbed for hanging with the Brooklyn K-9 Unit too much these days, Emmett filed a report and talked to his superiors regarding his cousin. He had permission to continue the hunt for Randall Gage, but he wouldn't overstep with the K-9 unit again.

He still had informants all around Brooklyn, so he expected one of them to alert him. But first, he had to see Belle and tell her how he felt.

He was on his way to do that when his phone buzzed.

Speaking of informants, Decker Palmer had been with him a long time. Emmett watched over Decker since the man was trying to get his life back together after losing a lot of money with gambling and stocks and then becoming an alcoholic. He lived in a halfway house in Bay Ridge. "What's up, Deck?"

"Hey, man, I saw your cuz about ten minutes ago. He was walking toward the apartment he used to live in—

the one in Bay Ridge you told me to watch. Only now it's a laundry or something. He looked real bad. I heard he's been hanging out at a homeless shelter nearby there."

"Thank you, Deck," Emmett said.

His informant hung up without another word.

Emmett put his truck in gear and turned around to head to Bay Ridge. If Randall was around, he intended to find him.

But he had to go by the book this time. So he called Gavin Sutherland and asked for assistance.

"I'll send Max Santelli and his K-9 Rottweiler, Sam. Sam's trained in suspect apprehension. A patrol officer will be with them."

Emmett had met Max once. He appeared intense and aggressive but was well liked, according to Belle. He gave Emmett the location. "Let me go in first and see if I can talk him into turning himself in."

"Okay, but…Max and Sam will be close by."

When Emmett arrived on the street where Randall had lived, Emmett parked his truck and started walking. Randall liked to hang out in diners since he never had gotten a good meal at home. Emmett's heart went out to his cousin. Randall had had a hard life, but that didn't give anyone the right to murder another human being. He wondered if the shelter had a soup kitchen.

He checked a few places but things had changed over the years. Finally, he saw a sign at the corner of 5th and 77th Street. Not far from the M-Train station.

Shelter from the Storm. Soup Kitchen All Day.

Emmett entered the building that had once been some sort of two-story retail store from the looks of it. Following the signs pointing to the kitchen, Emmett breathed a sigh of relief since the place wasn't packed with hungry people. He spotted Randall sitting alone in a worn arm-chair, watching an old Western. This time, he'd do things differently. He went in and sat down and looked over at his cousin. "Randall, don't run. I'll have to shoot you."

His cousin looked shocked to see Emmett and then he looked resigned. "Shooting me might be the best thing right now, man."

"I want to help you," Emmett said. "Let's walk out together, without any fuss, okay?"

"I haven't had breakfast," his cousin said, a stubborn gleam in his eyes.

Emmett leaned close. "Get it to go."

Randall shook his head and went to the open counter from the kitchen. "I need to get out of here. Can you wrap mine to go?"

The attendant nodded and brought him his food and gave him a to-go cup of coffee.

Emmett breathed a sigh of relief as they left the soup kitchen. He glanced around and spotted the NYPD cruiser parked up the street. "I'm not going to cuff you, but I'm going to take you to the Brooklyn K-9 Unit precinct," Emmett explained. "They want to ask you some questions regarding the McGregor murders twenty years ago."

Randall glared at him. "I didn't do anything, and I don't know what you're talking about."

Emmett could see the lies in his cousin's eyes. "Okay, then you shouldn't have anything to worry about."

They made it to the truck and Emmett moved to make sure his cousin got in. But Randall had other ideas. He whirled and threw hot coffee at Emmett. It hit his chest in a scalding fury, the bag of food following. The flimsy bag smashed into Emmett's face and fell to the ground, the bacon-and-egg sandwich splattering on the hot sidewalk.

Randall took off running.

The cruiser cranked and hurried up the street. Max came around the corner with a barking Sam.

Emmett knew the dog could apprehend and hold Randall, but he hesitated. "Max, bring Sam and follow me."

Emmett sprinted after Randall, his weapon drawn. He checked the street and watched helplessly as Randall swerved to the right into a crowded Starbucks. Emmett went in and searched. No Randall.

Then he turned and saw his cousin rushing out the door. Emmett pushed through the crowd and kept his eyes on Emmett as he hit the subway station.

And disappeared inside.

Max and his partner were right behind Emmett.

"I can track him from here," Max called.

Emmett took a breath. "Go."

Max took off toward the subway station and got lost in the crowd. Would he find Randall?

Emmett called in the report. "I had him, and he gave me the slip again. But Officer Santelli and Sam are in pursuit." He gave the location and the train route. What else could he do? He wasn't even supposed to be on this case.

And he didn't need to be on this case. He tried to never shoot in public places but with Randall, he'd hesitated twice now and twice his cousin had managed to get away.

I should have cuffed him right then and there.

It wouldn't happen again. He would pass this on to the people who were trying to find a killer. The Brooklyn K-9 Unit could finish their cold case without him.

Dejected, Emmett went back to his office and wrote up a report and then he called Gavin Sutherland and told him he was done.

"I should have cuffed him or at least held my weapon

on him but I was hoping he'd cooperate. I can see I'm too close to this. I'll stay out of the way from now on."

Gavin let out a huff of breath. "Relax. You did call for backup, but Randall got on the subway and they lost him. So it's not all your fault. The man knows his way around the streets of Brooklyn and he seems to have an uncanny ability to hide rather quickly. Don't beat yourself up, Marshal Gage."

"I'll try to remind myself that I do sometimes fail."

"And what about Officer Montera?" Gavin asked in that firm tone of his. "Are you going to fail at that?"

"I'm not done with Officer Montera yet, Sergeant Sutherland. That's between her and me."

"Fair enough," Gavin said. "I wish you the best, Marshal Gage."

"Will you keep me posted on Randall?" Emmett asked.

"Will you do the same for us?" Gavin countered.

"Of course."

"Then we'll call it even," Gavin said.

"You need to stop moping."

Belle gave Cara a stern stare and wished she'd stayed in her apartment. This family dinner would be full of questions. "I've had a long day. I can mope if I want to."

It had been two days since her ordeal. Two days and no word from Emmett.

This morning, she'd been called into the precinct to talk to Lieutenant Olivia Vance from Internal Affairs. Belle had to vouch for her colleague and friend Henry Roarke who was on modified desk duty. He had been accused of using excessive force when a twenty-year-old suspect had tried to grab Henry's weapon. With a body cam on the fritz, there was no proof of how things had gone down.

Olivia, a pretty but tough brunette, had taken over the

position when Lieutenant Jabboski had a mild heart attack. Belle, tired and irritated that her friend had to deal with this, had answered the lieutenant's pointed questions to the best of her ability. Now she was worried about Henry.

Detective Bradley McGregor, who'd been with Henry that night, had tried to assure Henry he'd be cleared. "I didn't see what happened but, man, I know you. No way. And I told that overly confident IA woman the same thing."

Belle had agreed with Bradley. "You're solid, Henry. Everyone knows that."

Henry's dark eyes had looked doubtful. Shaking his shaved head, he'd said, "Belle, you know the odds are against me."

Belle had touched his bronzed arm. "But you've beaten those odds over and over. Don't give up." Shrugging, she'd added, "Look at me. I've survived the worst."

That had made him smile. "And I thank you for coming in when you're supposed to be resting. I appreciate you, Belle."

She'd then slipped in and out of the precinct quickly because she hadn't wanted to answer any questions about Emmett and her.

But now Belle worried for her friend Henry and feared Emmett wouldn't ever come around again. Or maybe she was just letting her anxieties do their thing and run wild.

"It's not like you, though," her sister said while she shook out her still damp mane and then went back to folding napkins. "You got the bad guys and we're all safe again. It feels good. You're a hero, Belle."

Belle snapped back to attention. "I'm nobody's hero," she told Cara, following behind her with silverware for each place setting. "I got involved with the wrong man and made sure another abusive idiot went to jail. But they found each other and they both wanted revenge on me. That almost got me killed."

"But you survived and you fought back and maybe you found the right man," Anita chimed in, looking cute in a plaid tunic over black leggings. "Don't you think that's good for us to see?" Then she poked Belle's arm. "You are not the criminal, Belle. You went after the criminals and brought them down before the rescue team could get to you. You're kind of a big deal."

She needed to listen to her own advice. She'd reminded Henry of how she'd survived. He'd do the same. Henry was tough and always in control. Same as all of them.

"You're our role model," Anita said, grinning at her.

Belle reached her arms wide. "This role model loves you both." Her sisters hugged her and giggled.

"Don't tell me you're both going into law enforcement," she said as they finished putting her mother's meat loaf on the table.

"No, but I am," Joaquin said with a soft smile from where he stood pouring tea into their dinner glasses.

Mamá put her hands on her hips and whirled to stare at her son. "This is news to me."

"Is it true?" Papá asked, his eyes glistening with fear and pride. "Have you thought about this, Joaquin?"

"It's what I want," Joaquin said. "I don't have to think about it. I've lived through it but on the wrong side. I'm going to finish school and then I'm going to apply to attend the police academy."

Glancing at Belle, he said, "I hope you'll give me some pointers."

Belle's emotions shifted like a roller coaster. "I'd be happy to do that."

Their mother lapsed into Spanish, and not in a good way.

They all laughed and hugged her while she ranted on.

Finally, Joaquin grabbed his mother and gave her a big kiss. That won her over. She held him close, tears in her eyes. "I suppose I should be proud, *sí*?"

"*Sí,*" her children all retorted. Then they all rushed to find their seats.

The doorbell downstairs rang.

"I'll get it," Anita said. "And yes, I'll check the peephole first."

Belle went about passing potatoes and corn, thinking it was probably her uncle coming to check on them. He'd been so good about having the neighborhood watch members patrolling around their block.

But when she turned to see who Anita had brought up, her heart fluttered and came alive.

Emmett, with flowers and chocolate.

"Are those for me?" her mother deadpanned with a smile.

"No, ma'am, but I'm sure Belle will share with you," he replied.

Belle rushed to take the wildflowers and the box of chocolate. "Nice," she said. "Very nice."

"Cliché, but I was desperate," he whispered. "Can we talk?"

"First you eat," her mother announced, her tone undisputable.

Belle gave him a beseeching stare.

"I am hungry," he said with a grin. "Is that meat loaf?"

And so they ate, Belle's gaze hitting Emmett's when she thought no one was watching. But everyone was watching.

"So what's the deal with you two?" Cara asked in her sassy way.

"Cara!" Her sister gave her a be-quiet glare. Then Anita turned to Belle and Emmett. "But...we all want to know."

Belle stood. "That's it. Marshal Gage and I are going downstairs to my apartment for some privacy."

"We'll want details," her mother said, shoving two dessert plates at them. "Coconut cake."

Emmett took the plates with another grin. "I could get used to this."

After they were in Belle's apartment with the dead bolt on, he took their dessert plates and put them on the counter. Then he turned to face her.

Pulling her into his arms, he said, "Hi."

"Hi," she replied. "I missed you."

"I had to figure out some things," he replied, his hand moving through her hair.

"About us?"

"No, I've pretty much decided that I'm in love with you."

Belle's heart did a little dance, a mixture of awareness and anticipation. "That's good, because I've pretty much decided I'm in love with you, too."

"I can get used to that, too," he said, kissing her.

Belle enjoyed the kiss and then lifted her head back. "But...you have to deal with Randall."

"I did try to deal with him again yesterday," he told her. "But he got away again."

She listened while he filled her in. "Emmett, I'm so sorry. It must be hard, knowing he's the only family you have left around here. I think it's good that you're stepping away."

Emmett's eyes held hers, the misery in his words showing in his expression. "I have to step away, but I won't stop thinking about him or hoping he'll do the right thing. But I can't be the one to bring him in. I'm too close."

"I understand," she said. "But this won't be in our way, will it?"

Emmett looked into her eyes. "You mentioned my not having family here, but Belle, when I'm with you and your family, I feel at home. I think I've found my people, my person. I want to be with you."

"And my family?" she asked, tears in her eyes.

"Yes, oh, yes." He lifted her and twirled her around. "I get meat loaf and coconut cake. Are you kidding me?"

Belle laughed while Justice woofed a happy bark.

"And you get me, Marshal Gage."

"That's the best part of all." He touched his finger to her chin. "I want to marry you and come home to you and get in arguments with your siblings and…be here to guide them and help them. I want to spend the rest of my life with you."

Belle kissed him and then said, "We'll need the rest of this floor."

"For our family?"

"Yes." She ruffled his hair. "For our family."

"I might have rescued you that day in the park," Emmett said, "but you saved me."

Then he kissed her again before they both dug into their cake and smiled at each other.

Justice sighed and sank down on his haunches. His work here was done.

* * * * *

Look for Henry Roarke's story, Explosive Situation, *by Terri Reed, the next book in the True Blue K-9 Unit: Brooklyn series, available in July 2020.*

True Blue K-9 Unit: Brooklyn
These police officers fight for justice with the help of their brave canine partners.

Copycat Killer
by Laura Scott, April 2020

Chasing Secrets
by Heather Woodhaven, May 2020

Deadly Connection
by Lenora Worth, June 2020

Explosive Situation
by Terri Reed, July 2020

Tracking a Kidnapper
by Valerie Hansen, August 2020

Scene of the Crime
by Sharon Dunn, September 2020

Cold Case Pursuit
by Dana Mentink, October 2020

Delayed Justice
by Shirlee McCoy, November 2020

True Blue K-9 Unit Christmas: Brooklyn
by Laura Scott and Maggie K. Black,
December 2020

Dear Reader

I hope you enjoyed this K-9 story set in Brooklyn. I'll admit I didn't know much about Brooklyn, New York, when I started this book but I loved finding some of the beautiful spots in this part of New York City and seeing my characters come alive on the pages. It's always a challenge to write about death and crime, especially in a place you've only passed through while going to the airport.

But we always strive to make our K-9 stories as authentic as possible while maintaining a wholesome love story. I hope I hit that mark with Emmett and Belle. I loved Belle's big family but I also ached for Emmett, who seemed so alone in the world. I grew up in a large Southern family, so while I was a fish out of water, I identified with some of the issues Belle had to deal with. This is an exciting series and I'm happy to be a part of it. I hope you're enjoying it, too.

Until next time, may the angels watch over you. Always

Lenora

WE HOPE YOU ENJOYED
THIS BOOK FROM

LOVE INSPIRED SUSPENSE
INSPIRATIONAL ROMANCE

Courage. Danger. Faith.

Find strength and determination in stories
of faith and love in the face of danger.

6 NEW BOOKS AVAILABLE EVERY MONTH!

SPECIAL EXCERPT FROM

LOVE INSPIRED SUSPENSE
INSPIRATIONAL ROMANCE

*After months of searching, security expert Ryker Tillman
finally finds Olivia Habush and her young son—just
as they are attacked by armed mercenaries. Now
safeguarding Olivia, her unborn child and little Aaron is
the former special ops soldier's new mission.*

*Read on for a sneak preview of
Guarded by the Soldier by Laura Scott,
available in July 2020 from Love Inspired Suspense.*

Something was very wrong.

"Stay behind me." Ryker gently but firmly pushed
Olivia behind him. "Where's your son's room?" he asked
in a whisper.

"Upstairs next to mine," she whispered back.

He nodded and made his way down the short hallway
to the two bedrooms separated by a tiny bathroom. One
bedroom door was open; the other was closed.

With his foot, he shoved the door hanging ajar all the
way open. The room was vacant. Testing the knob of the
closed bedroom door, he found it wasn't locked. Keeping
Olivia behind him, he abruptly shoved the door open,
then stepped back to wait.

Nothing happened. Ryker cautiously crossed the
threshold, then stopped abruptly when he saw the older
woman lying on the bed.

The nanny was dead.

"Willa!" Olivia's horrified gasp indicated she knew the woman was gone. "Oh, no! Where's Aaron?"

"Olivia, please," he tried but then he heard the sound of someone coming down the stairs. "Run away and call for help."

"Not without my son!"

"Go!" He pushed Olivia toward the door then quickly but silently crossed the living room into the kitchen, flipping the light off as he went. There was a side doorway that he felt certain led up to the second-story apartment.

He took up a defensive position behind the door and waited, hoping the guy who likely had Aaron didn't know that his cohort in crime had failed at kidnapping Olivia.

"Mommy! Mommy! I want my mommy!" Aaron's cries echoed high and shrill above the thumping footsteps coming down the stairs.

"Aaron! I'm here, baby, don't worry!" Olivia's voice rang out loudly and Ryker momentarily closed his eyes, wishing he'd handled things differently.

He should have gotten Olivia and Aaron out of the city the moment he'd found them.

Instead he may have caused the very thing he'd been trying to avoid.

Getting them both killed.

Don't miss
Guarded by the Soldier *by Laura Scott,*
available July 2020 wherever
Love Inspired Suspense books and ebooks are sold.

LoveInspired.com

LISEXP0620